MW00932271

OCT -2 2020

D R Toi
223 Southlake Pl
Newport News, VA 23602-8323

COSMIC WANDERERS
Homeward Bound

Jasmuheen

Enchanted Kingdom Series with Jasmuheen

Book 1 - *Queen of the Matrix – Fiddlers of the Field* – the alchemical apprenticeship begins. Also covers future artificial intelligence issues.

Book 2 - *King of Hearts – The Field of Love* – covers the complicated alchemy of human relationships and love from an interdimensional level.

Book 3 - *Elysium – Shamballa's Sacred Symphony* – explores the alchemy of love, duality and the more enlightened planes.

Book 4 - *Cosmic Wanderers – Homeward Bound* – goes deeper into the ancient and futuristic alchemy of an ascending species and world.

It is not necessary to have read the previous books
in the Enchanted Kingdom series, to enjoy and appreciate
all that this new book in the E.K. series contains.

When the Queen of the Matrix,
returns the King to her heart,
peace will come to all on Earth,
regardless of their part.
And when compassion sets the pace,
Earth's people will find new rhythm,
a peace within, and a peace without,
to last beyond millenniums.
Elysium Prophecy

First published in September 2012
by the

SELF EMPOWERMENT ACADEMY
P.O. Box 1754, Buderim, 4556
Queensland, Australia
Fax: +61 7 5445 6075

www.selfempowermentacademy.com.au
www.jasmuheen.com

ISBN: 978-1-300-24344-1

The Enchanted Kingdom Series:-
Queen of the Matrix – Fiddlers of the Fields
King of Hearts – The Field of Love
Elysium – Shamballa's Sacred Symphony
Cosmic Wanderers – Homeward Bound

http://www.lulu.com/spotlight/jasmuheen

Once upon a time
there was the dreaming,
where dreamers created worlds
that they longed for.
And in the dreaming and the longing,
new worlds were born,
for the dreamers knew the magic
to reweave the webs of life.

DEDICATION

Special dedication to our
interdimensional family of Light.

~ 1 ~

Marselan

Marselan was deep in thought, a tall solitary figure, bearded and tanned, who was currently feeling a little brittle and barely aware of his surroundings. There was talk among the Tribunal of yet another war in the Betelgeuse system. In Orion, their struggles seemed endless and he realized how tired he was of it all; tired of Tribunals and tired of talk of war. His left leg was aching as he trudged along the cliff tops oblivious to the late afternoon sun that was finally beginning to stream through overcast skies. It had been raining all day, which had added to his already melancholy mood.

His limb began to throb, still not completely healed yet he was managing to walk further each day and of this he felt proud. He stopped then bent over to slowly massage his thigh, feeling the ridge of the rough sutures where he'd recently stitched his own gaping wounds. The warfare had been bloody, their casualties high and still it raged somewhere above him in a far off cosmic sky.

Marselan sat propped up against a rocky outcrop, sighed deeply and thought, *Perhaps I've grown too old for war.* He'd come from Orion's more positive Clarion planetary system, which had long known peace but his work as an Emissary often took him far away.

Peace was in his blood, was what he fought for.

What a contradiction, he'd often mused to himself, *to fight for peace …*

Marselan saw it then as he looked up and glanced out across the ocean, aware of the dolphin's high-pitched call. They were nudging a mass of something in towards the shore. He extended his mind out to them and sensed it was a body, unconscious but still with a faint breath of life. Scrambling down the steep escarpment trying to hurry but not fall, he cursed the war for his injuries, which took away his natural grace then realized that at least he was alive. While his Starship crew fought valiantly on without him, he was able to recuperate upon his favorite isle and for this, he was thankful.

Breathless by the time he reached the woman's body that was now beached upon the shore; he winced in pain as he bent low over her form, then sent a quick thought of thanks out to the dolphins who swam playfully away knowing their delivery had been made. The baby they knew that was alive in the young woman's womb was safe.

Marselan felt the slow pulse in her neck then worked quickly to clear her airways, giving her mouth to mouth, before turning her gently over to expel the last of the water from her lungs. He was amazed she was still alive and wondered from where she had come. The young woman coughed then spluttered but didn't open her eyes and instead began to shiver, her wet swimwear providing no protection from the rising wind as summer's night began to fall.

He wrapped her in his oversized shirt to shield her from the breeze and then scooped her up into his arms to carry her close to his chest, only to sense her slip into a deep coma-like sleep. He glanced down at her in awe as he slowly wound his way back up the overgrown path that he knew the ancients had once used upon this Isle, his Avalon where no one ever came. Marselan was usually alone here but never lonely – at least not until today when he felt a strange sensation of happiness to have found her.

Struggling up the incline, he began to feel unsteady on his legs and his breathing suddenly became erratic as his heartbeat fast in his chest. He stopped for a moment and took a few deep breaths. Still clutching the dark haired woman in his arms, he looked back across the island with its long expanse of beach and thought how beautiful it was, a sacred place just for him that no one else had been to for so long. He always came to the island to heal, for his wounds had been numerous over the years of intergalactic struggle in his people's bid for peace. Coming here allowed him time to tune out from it all and to rest and think.

Many from the Orion constellation were more generally known for their aggressive nature, for their desire to colonize other worlds, for their hunger for resources and for their political resolve and the alliances, they formed. Few knew of the planets there that were of a more positive nature, those inhabited by the ones who'd finally grown spiritually enough to become more conscious with their creation.

All of this Marselan dwelt on now as he began again to struggle up the steep incline in front of the rock wall that shielded his cottage from the often-windblown beach. The tides had brought in many things of interest but never another human. Few from Earth's realm could even see this little island that existed in another dimension within the Tyrrhenian Sea.

He pushed open the front door then laid her gently on the big warm rug beside the fire on his hearth before sitting back on his haunches and closing his eyes to scan her body and energy form. It was then that he felt the baby's heartbeat so closely following her own as if they beat together, synchronized in a sacred rhythm. As he passed his hand over her brow, he felt a blackness consuming her mind and knew she'd have no memory when she woke. And so he searched deeper into her being to find from which star system she'd come, for one such as her could never have been brought by the dolphins to his shores unless she was a more recent Star-borne.

Moments later he opened his eyes in shock as her memories flooded through him of a time long past. He saw her violet hue and what she'd agreed to do long before coming through space and time to take embodiment on Earth. To Marselan she was a kindred spirit, loving, kind and free, now lost and alone, literally cast adrift upon Earth's sea.

I wonder if she knows of this, where she's from this time? he thought about her ancient past as he wiped the sweat from her brow before a fever fully set in. He closed his eyes again and moved a few days back in time where he saw her lying on top of a surfboard enjoying the stillness of a peaceful retreat. He watched her lazy smile as she drifted unintentionally off to sleep, relaxed and unaware as a strong current carried her out, and then across a deep green sea.

Who loves you little one? Marselan thought as he wrapped her in soft white blankets. *You are well loved, that I can feel, well missed and mourned for, no doubt about that at all ... and ... well, if you were mine, I'd never let you out of my sight to be lost at all.*

As dawn broke, he sat down near where she lay and gently extended his mind once more to connect to the baby within her, only to find a son with months left still to grow before it would be born. *So my little man, I wonder why the winds of fate have sent you both to my door?*

And so the woman before him slept and dreamed safe by Marselan's fire. In her dream, she'd slipped off a long, flat board and plunged deep into the sea ... been drowning ... couldn't breathe ... was gasping for air and her struggle for life seemed to go on forever. Then the dream changed and she was floating safely on her back, being nudged along by the dolphin-pod who had quickly sensed her baby and her fear.

Next she was drifting again alone but calm on top of a gentle sea. Dolphins cavorted around her, chattering with excitement, nudging her now and then to flip her over or to move her forward. She felt languid and resigned as if the tides of life were purposefully carrying her in a different direction, away from the life she'd planned.

She didn't resist and the current was strong. She rested; lay on her back with her hands behind her head as the dream carried her along. It all felt surreal, as if she were being delivered to someone and to some place that she'd once belonged. All she felt was stillness and a sense of peace.

Her body shuddered and sighed and she slipped further into sleep to live in another dream aboard the Starship called Elysium. In this dream, she found herself in a sacred chamber seated lotus style before an Ancient Elder.

"It is written," he said softly with a loving twinkle in his eyes. "A new life for you all. To the past you must now say goodbye." And with the wizard's words something within her let go and she began to drift, floating through the cosmos away from the Starship and all that it contained.

~ 2 ~

Marselan sat straight backed and focused upon the mountain behind his cottage; sending out his telepathic call, tuning to the Starship that he knew now hovered somewhere in space above him. His leg was throbbing again and he placed his hand upon it willing the cells to reassemble themselves back to health, instructing his body to strengthen as green light flowed from his palm into the wound. He could feel his body drinking in the light as it came in through the doorway of his psychic heart then cascaded down his arm into his palm to irradiate his leg. It had never taken so long to heal before but then he had never been so heart weary regarding war.

Unable to make contact with the craft, Marselan grew restless, unwilling to focus, not caring anymore and so he came back to the cottage to sit on the floor beside her bed. He felt despondent, more so since she'd come, the strange young beauty who been washed up on his shore.

How long had it been since her arrival? He'd lost track of time, for time didn't matter where he was now, and somehow the passing of time slowed right down on the Island, until it seemed to stop existing at all. One day here was the same as three or four days in the outer world. He also knew that his healing always took as long as it took but then there was healing of not just body but also of heart and mind.

As he sat on the floor beside her bed, he tuned into the energy fields of the other islands around him, to sense the grief of those who may be looking for her as what he had gained someone else had lost. The islands felt shielded from him and a small voice rose within him that said, *"She has returned, just accept that finally she has been returned."* Before he could clarify this gentle inner message, the woman turned in her sleep and the sheet fell away from her body to reveal a lithe, strong form.

How long will it be until she wakes? he wondered as he checked her pulse and dehydration levels and realized her body was able to feed itself, in the cosmic way, from prana. He too could be nourished in this way and so were all his men. It was a good freedom for them all to

13

have, to take physical food only for the pleasure and not the need. He gazed at her face wondering where she'd been trained but received no more intuitive insight except that despite her obvious good health, her coma seemed deep. It was as if her body longed for nothing but sleep and with the passing of each day all Marselan longed for was to see her eyes.

A few days later at dusk, it happened.

As he placed fresh fruit upon the table, he felt her gaze upon his back and heard her calmly whisper, "Thank you." He turned to her slowly, his heart beating faster than a drum as a joy flooded into his chest.

Emerald, her eyes are emerald with a few blue flecks. Add long dark hair, olive skin and she looks like a Goddess from the stars, young but not too young for me. Oh God what am I thinking? he reflected as he took in her physical appearance. *She's pregnant and probably already in love with someone, definitely loved well by someone ...*

"I'd introduce myself," she said softly, "but I can't seem to remember anything ... except that it seems like I've been asleep forever drifting among the stars and that you don't feel like a stranger ... do I know you?" She appeared a touch perplexed and yet complacent, unalarmed.

"Marselan," he intoned pointing to his chest. "Found you with the dolphins near the beach, they helped you in."

"I dreamt I was floating in the sea ..."

"It wasn't a dream."

"Ahh ..." was all she said.

"You remember nothing more?"

"Nothing, at least not yet," she said then suddenly feeling thirsty smiled and held out the empty cup beside her bed.

As he limped over to fill her glass, she noticed the way he dragged his leg and a questioning look filled her face.

"War wounds ..."

"From?"

He pointed to the night sky towards the direction of the Orion constellation.

"Intergalactic warfare?"

"How did you know?"

"Didn't, guessed, you have that warrior-man look about you." She liked him she decided, he looked tough but tender hearted, cool but caring. She tried to sit up but she felt too shaky and immediately slumped back down.

"Careful, remember the baby ..."

"Baby? I'm pregnant?"

"No wedding band that I noticed but definitely pregnant," he grinned.

"How do you know?"

"Scanned you for injuries when you arrived, sensed a few things about you but we can talk about this later, you look tired ..."

"Not yet ready to go back to sleep," she yawned. "Need answers," she added yawning again.

"Told you the important things for now," he smiled, delighted by everything about her.

"Okay, well, then, so that's about it regarding me, that I have no memory, a baby in the belly and dolphin friends in the sea. So who are you?"

"Told you, Marselan. Galactic warrior from the Orion constellation, the Clarion system actually. Peace Emissary on leave but right now more like a wounded bear. Also friend of dolphins. There you have it all."

"Oh I doubt that," she managed to tease, "so where exactly are we? Still on Earth I see?"

"Sort of. Avalon, as I call this island, is kind of in a twilight zone, generally not seen by any unless they have the gift." He helped her settle back down sensing her body's need for more sleep then added gently, "Relax, we have lots of talk time before us, that I can assure you, as there's no way off this island for a while. Time also slows down here in the most unusual way. One last thing ..."

"Mmmm?" she muttered as she felt her body's strong desire for sleep.

"What's your favorite name? The one you'd give a daughter?"

"I'm having a girl?"

"No, I think it's a son, but you need a name until you remember your own."

"Sarah."

"Then that's what I will call you." Marselan smiled as she drifted off again to sleep.

She dreamt of places and faces that filled her with great love, a mother with a grown son who she loved more like a lover than a brother, and to them she said goodbye. Their parting was poignant and tender, filled with a knowing that the tides of life had moved them on.

In her dream, she moved into a brand new future where she played on an island with her young son and the man into whose life she had come.

As the new dreamscape settled, Marselan came to her gently, stepping fully into this part of her dream as if he'd always belonged. Bending down he caressed her face and as he rested his index finger on her third eye, hundreds of scenes flashed between them of their life in another time, in a far off galaxy before she came to Earth.

"Oh my beloved," he sighed as they embraced and her heart was filled with a feeling of peace that was so profound. She was home again, of that, she could be sure and while none of this dream would be remembered, in her heart she knew.

She awoke from the dream to the warmth of sunlight bathing her body and face and the smell of coffee on the stove. The cottage felt rustic, unlived in yet it had a feel to it as if it was where she belonged. She had no reason to be anywhere and felt strangely complacent about both her amnesia and the man she knew who had found her.

"You seem unusually calm," Marselan later noted as they sat enjoying the afternoon sun after a leisurely lunch of nuts and fruits.

"I don't see what choice I have," Sarah noted pragmatically. "There's not much I can do without my memory and for some strange reason I feel as if the past doesn't even matter ... I know I should probably feel stressed or worried but I don't. I'm pregnant. Someone out there must be looking for me. Maybe even love me but I feel nothing … except that I should be here with you now …" she blushed and looked away as Marselan confirmed he thought the same.

They talked for hours sharing as if they were long time companions until suddenly Marselan looked pensive. "There's something you should know, things I saw in your memory pool when I scanned your system to see how the baby was doing. I didn't mean to pry and I must admit to being thrown by what I encountered …"

"Which was?"

"Just that in another timeline we knew each other quite well."

"How well?" she smiled feeling strangely pleased by his admission.

"Well enough for us both to feel extremely comfortable with each other now," he grinned, looking and feeling more youthful by the moment. His skin was olive like hers, his hair was touched by a few slivers of grey and his blue eyes held the look of someone who'd discovered many things.

"You shaved off your beard," she said as she reached out and gently touched his face in a gesture that felt familiar to them both. "I like it," she stated matter-of-factly then added, "so when do I get the guided tour of your island?"

"Five miles long, two miles wide, one tall mountain, plus a few hidden valleys that hold doorways to other realms, I think the island will give you its own tour soon enough." At this, she raised her eyebrow and so he added, "Okay, just let me rest my leg for a few more days then I'll show you what I've found on my island abode. Anything else here will no doubt reveal itself to you in time."

~ 3 ~

Matthias

The craft was sleek, well designed, comfortable and compact. The distances they'd travelled throughout the cosmos the last month astounded him. Matthias felt as if he was awake within a dream as childhood desires for intergalactic travel were fulfilled beyond his wildest yearnings.

Commander Inshallah.

The name set well upon him.

Ambassador Matthias Inshallah. He liked this too.

It seemed like yesterday since contact with the Elysium had been made and that he'd established the Embassy on Earth with Isabella soon stepping in to work at his side. So much has been accomplished in such a short time, consuming his attention and making him feel passionate again about life.

Isabella had survived the assassination attempt in Vienna, so had Tao Lao and the president to be who was now officially ensconced in office. Isabella had mourned Yesif, he knew, just as he still mourned the passing of his own wife, for both had been struck down before their time; Yesif by an assassin's bullet and Inshallah's wife by the silent cancer that had slowly consumed her. Without his work with 8tlan and Tao Lao, Matthias knew he'd never have survived for the pain of his loss would have been too much to bear.

He missed her, craved her touch and smile. He never knew he could feel so empty yet so full at the same time; empty with the missing of his wife and full at the passion of his Ambassadry and the recent exploration of the interdimensional worlds. He felt exhilarated by it all, slightly overwhelmed.

Tao Lao had taught him well these last few years and his assistant Isabella was naturally gifted. She'd slotted into his life like another daughter, full of calm and grace; regal and open, caring and compassionate like a queen. She was a little too young for his personal romantic interest and besides he'd had one great love already and wasn't sure if he'd ever be open for more. *Maybe someone like 8tlan, when the time is right,* he thought about the Starship Elysium's commander. *Tao Lao's a lucky man* ... formidable, intelligent, and beautiful, 8tlan was all of this and more ... but then so was Tao Lao. They were the perfect couple to be sure.

As the small starship moved through the interdimensional fields, Matthias let his mind wander back through the past to reflect on how well Tao Lao had trained him and how he'd done it by example rather than words.

He recalled that fateful day in Vienna where Yesif had been groomed to set off his bomb and take the lives of so many others around him. How the youth had seen Isabella, his uncle Joseph and Tao Lao seated in the audience so close to where his target was speaking, the young black woman touted to be president within the coming years. But Yesif had walked out, succumbing to his conscience to save the ones he loved. It was Tao Lao who had sensed the snipers on the roof as the Dark Ones backup plan. The monk had saved them all, but not before the bullets had sprayed out, missing one of their marks but taking out the other. Brave yet humble, Tao Lao's courage was evident for all to see and now he was back in the Middle East helping to refine the Peace Treaties.

"Father?"

Matthias looked up, his reminiscing disturbed by the gentle presence of his daughter. She was a walking contradiction; tough and strong but sweet and gently confidant yet sometimes withdrawn and shy.

"Time to land?"

"Ten minutes," she confirmed knowing he always loved to watch their re-entry through the stratosphere of Earth. *Thank God for Isabella,* he thought, as he watched his daughter strap herself in. She still looked haunted and unsettled yet lately color had begun to fill her face and her eyes looked a little less sad due to Isabella's friendship and concern.

"We'll call her Celestia," his wife had pronounced the day their daughter was born, a strange little gift from the stars that came to them long after they'd surrendered the hope of ever having a child.

"You are pleased?" Celestia enquired as the small, sleek craft completed its landing process and they prepared to disembark on the Embassy rooftop.

"Pleased? I suppose I am." Then he added with a gentle smile, "For a first meeting it was successful, more was achieved than I'd hoped."

"They made you a Commander within the Federation, put the Embassy and yourself at the forefront as one of Earth's main representatives in future dealings with them. Many will be ecstatic with this news."

"As am I Celestia," Matthias responded feeling so enlivened by what had occurred.

"And now?"

"We rest, then I need to talk with both Tan and Isabella and fill them in on our news."

"Where is Isabella now? I've missed her ..."

"Still fine-tuning her diplomatic skills, providing back-up to Tao Lao, nothing like hands-on learning," he stated with a grin, then added brightly, "hopefully she'll be back soon, speaking of the formidable young woman, have you heard anything from Angel?"

"No all is silent of that front ... she'll contact us soon, when she's ready ..."

Matthias nodded, then brightened, "By the way I had no idea you could fly like that! Your previous training on board the Elysium has given you many skills."

"I'm just thankful Tan allowed us to take his craft and trusted that I could fly it."

Celestia's face lit up with his name and Matthias realized that his daughter had fallen in love.

~ 4 ~

Tan

Celestia looked up at Tan shyly, her long dark hair partially covering her face leaving one big eye to lazily drink him in and then she looked away. He had noticed her staring, a strange look upon her face as if she was hesitant to connect. She reminded him of Rani.

It was less painful now although his loss of Rani was like a dull ache that had been permanently anchored into a corner of his heart. It used to consume him but the pain had gradually lessened. With the passing of time, Tan's heart had slowly healed as resignation turned into acceptance, although the light of hope that she could still be alive had never diminished entirely. They'd done everything they could to find her but she'd simply vanished.

His surrogate mother Mary, had refused to accept that her beloved daughter had gone although she, like Tan, had slowly learnt to smile again and greet each day as if every moment was precious, as if life had only just begun. Her life partner Jacob, had encouraged Mary to take a long sabbatical, as her heart was no longer in her work since Rani's disappearance. She spent her days painting, taking long walks by the sea on the opposite side of the world from where the ocean had taken her Rani away. She grew flowers and walked the hills on the old property that she had fallen in love with on the Eastern coast of Australia, near Byron Bay. Their property was close to Mount Warning and the Lamington National Park plateau, a land mass that was more than 55 million years old where U.F.O sightings were common.

Tan knew that Mary's life couldn't have been more different than the one she'd lived in Paris and yet she seemed content. Happy with country life and being with Jacob, Mary rarely travelled any more preferring instead to quietly do her energy work on the inner planes. Each time Tan spoke to her, Mary spoke as if Rani was still alive for in Mary's heart she was.

"I would know," she'd told him. "I would know if Rani had died. She'd come in my dreams and tell me, I'm sure she's come in yours, hasn't she?"

"Only once where I remember the details," Tan had said, then paused before quietly adding, "in that dream she'd come to say goodbye. I can't feel her energy around me anywhere and if she was alive I'm sure I would ..."

"Well I do," Mary had interjected. "I feel her alive in my heart."

"How's Jacob?" Tan then asked needing to change the conversation. And so they had talked on, but that was weeks ago.

Rani, Tan still couldn't believe that she was gone, still didn't believe that she had drowned for they'd never found her body. She didn't feel dead to him either but how long did one wait before picking up the pieces of a broken heart and moving on?

He had dreamt of her from time to time but not since she'd come and said her poignant goodbye. Was it a dream or did she really come as if to give him permission to let go of the life they'd planned.

The Heartland Game that they'd created had been released in video form. This gave them financial independence, yet her share of the profits remained untouched. Mary had been her beneficiary and she'd refused to spend a cent, saying Rani may need it whenever she returned.

Rani's many faces loomed before him now, plus a kaleidoscope of forms; Rani as a child in the Enchanted Kingdom, suffering in the witch's cellar with Seth, their escape and return to Mary's world. Their time in the jungles with Tao Lao where they learnt the ways of the Shaman, and then the time when they'd entered into Hosho's realm.

Tan recalled their training aboard the Cadets Space Station with Loki and Aphrodite; how he and Rani had slowly fallen in love after she realized that Tan was not her brother at all. He remembered her disappearance into the Shadowlands, his anger, and then her return, then his own beating and coma. He would have died then if he had been without her for only Rani could have brought him back to life to finish the Heartland Game. When finally he thought that all their hard times were done and a new chapter had begun, she'd disappeared again.

He was tired he realized, tired of all of their dramas. He was also tired of missing her, and tired of missing what had been.

His relationship with Rani had never been easy except when they were children. Once they'd grown and realized that they were not blood related, everything had changed. Emotionally damaged by the warlock Seth, Rani was unable to trust or love yet when she had finally opened up to him, Tan himself had been lost in their love.

He didn't want this anymore, he realized. He wanted his heart to be free of her, filled again with joy and peace. And now Inshallah's daughter had come.

Tan refocused himself back into the present moment and stared at Celestia wondering what it was about her, what had caught his eye, all the while feeling a subtle energy current between them.

Celestia glanced at him again, saw his look and felt the sadness in his soul, then nodded and excused herself from the room; leaving the softest scent of her jasmine perfume behind. She smelt like Rani, walked like her as well, with her long tanned limbs and agile grace.

Her father watched Tan watching Celestia then smiled and felt that a match had been made. Matthias knew he'd never have a better son-in-law than Tan. He also sensed that marriage and being bonded again in love was the farthest thing from Tan's mind; yet Matthias knew the look in his daughter's eye and that it wouldn't be long until Tan succumbed.

"Matthias," Tan acknowledged.

"Tan."

"All is progressing nicely I am told."

"A few incidents of mistrust but nothing unexpected considering how our governments have dealt with the extraterrestrial phenomena in the past. As you know, the constant negative portrayal in the movies of aliens taking over the Earth hasn't helped relations either." Matthias smiled then added gently: "My daughter seems to have taken a shine to you … most unusual I must say."

Intrigued, Tan asked him why.

"She tends to keep to herself these days especially since her mother passed on."

"Sorry to hear that ..."

"It's been awhile, we've adjusted ... as much as you can when you lose the one you love," Matthias responded sadly.

Tan didn't know what to say. Words always failed him in times like this when he saw someone's heart so raw. Words never seemed adequate anymore and so he looked behind Matthias to the huge computer screen and all it contained. Charts, diagrams and an updated mission statement lit up via an interactive computer that responded to their voices.

"Ah, you've noticed," Matthias confirmed then brightened, "yes it's the same screen and diagnostics as you have on board the Starship Elysium. As you know Tao Lao and 8tlan helped us set it up shortly after contact was first made. Perfect model, incredible technology, doubt anything on Earth can match it!"

Years had passed since that fateful day when 8tlan revealed the presence of the Starship in Earth's skies. At least a year had passed since Rani had been taken, swept out to sea on what had been a sun-filled day. A strong swimmer, it seemed that she'd failed to negotiate the deadly currents and tides.

Tan felt the familiar pain and longing in his heart, its icy tendrils squeezing the hurt that was stored there until it spread throughout his body. He felt raw again, exposed and suddenly unable to breath, he rose and excused himself from the room.

They collided in the corridor, both absorbed in the silent world of their own pain. As Celestia stumbled back against the wall, Tan reached out to cushion her fall, scooping her quickly up into his capable arms.

Celestia relaxed, leant into him, breathlessly apologizing in a low and richly timbered voice that spoke to his deepest core.

"Sorry, so clumsy these days, my mind always seems to be a million miles away ..." her voice trailed off as if she was silently chiding herself and her lack of focus. "Used to be so focused and present, don't know where I am anymore."

"Interdimensional travel can do that," he conceded, breathing in the scent of her, feeling how perfectly she fit into his arms, amazed that he could feel any of this at all.

"Thanks," she muttered then drew back and gave Tan a smile that made her suddenly radiant. An unexpected surge of feeling filled his heart and soul, a tingle of protective affection with a hint of something more.

"Better get back to our meeting," she whispered in a husky voice that Tan thought belied her tender years. Maybe she was older than she looked.

"Right behind you," he muttered, surprised at his body's response. It had been a long time since he'd even noticed another woman or held one in his arms. With her big, bright eyes and finely chiseled features, Celestia was strangely beautiful with a voice like nectar, designed to soothe his soul.

~ 5 ~

"So Ambassador Inshallah, where were we?" Tan enquired as he re-entered the Embassy's conference room with Celestia and sat back down.

Matthias breathed deeply, unsure where to begin, or if he even believed all that he'd been told. Tan had been trained by Hosho, he'd crossed the lines of time, had travelled extensively throughout the interdimensional planes; Tan he trusted just as he trusted Tan's first mentor Tao Lao but the ancient monk was unreachable again so Tan would have to do. Besides, this was Tan's job, to be a go-between, an emissary between the Embassy and 8tlan's realm.

"You looked concerned … I'd hoped the trip was a success for you?" Tan queried.

"It was more than a success! There's just so much to digest, things I need to discuss with you but I'm not sure where to begin …"

"Your new commission? As Commander with the Federation representing Earth? That fits well?"

"Like a glove," Matthias grinned, his eyes filling with delight at the opportunities offered and revealed.

"Then what?" Tan asked and patiently waited for Matthias to begin.

The elder statesman glanced at his daughter unsure of what she needed to hear then remembered their code of no secrets. She was twenty-eight now, a woman not a girl, a suitable match for Tan. They were in this together, there would be no turning back, still he'd become unsettled by all that he'd recently heard.

Matthias collected his thoughts and tentatively began, "What do you know of the Orion constellation?"

"Apart from the fact that some of their planets are warlike and some are at peace?" Tan responded.

"Yes, what else have you gleaned in your travels?"

"The territories seem well defined I'm told. All say 'as below, so above' meaning that just as Earth has had her battles and struggles with darkness and light so too have other systems within the multiverses. In your world many are still grasping the concept 'as above so below' yet the reverse I have found is also true … philosophically speaking …"

"But Orion specifically," Matthias interrupted. "Isn't that where the Volcan Lords originated from?"

"Many think so," Tan responded, happy to no longer be involved with the Dark Ones and their spread of fear. Earth had been more peaceful for a while. "What exactly do you need confirmed here Ambassador?"

Matthias remained silent as if lost in contemplation and then he cleared his throat and spoke.

"I know that the Intergalactic Federation is benevolent, that it comprises of beings of light from the higher dimensions, from the Pleiades, Vega, Lyra and Sirius systems, plus the Peace Lords from Venus and Arcturus. I know that many of these Light Beings have overseen Earth's evolution for thousands of years, at least according to Indigenous legends, but what I was recently told on this last journey I must admit has caused some consternation …" he paused then and so Tan asked:

"Surely Tao Lao and 8tlan briefed you on this when contact was first made?"

"They did," Matthias confirmed then became almost wishful, "I guess I just felt that in the interdimensional realms that all was light and love, civilized, filled with beings who understood Universal Law and how to use it wisely."

"It is on many levels …" Tan responded.

"But not all?"

"No, not all. Just because some star systems are technologically advanced, some hundreds of years beyond Earth's technical abilities, doesn't mean they are all driven by the desire to honor the highest good," Tan clarified.

"So it seems …"

"I assume then that you have just learnt now of the Orion grays?"

"And the Draconian Forces …"

"Of which the Volcan Lords are a part," Tan stated.

"Is it true what else some say about them?" Matthias queried. Keeping his eyes on Tan, he then added, "That Earth isn't even ours to begin with? That our species has been genetically manipulated by some, encoded later by others? That Earth is being fought over right now despite all our efforts for a peaceful merging?"

Tan sat back in his seat, watched the look of surprise dawn on Celestia's face as she took in what her father was saying.

"Well?" Matthias and Celestia asked in unison both now focused on Tan.

"There are stories," Tan began, unsure why Matthias was so agitated and unsettled, then realizing that information was power and that one of the Ambassador's roles was to keep many others well informed. "I guess that the idea of supreme races of extraterrestrial intelligence manipulating human evolution genetically is probably too much for many to handle but to be honest, I've never paid any of this too much focus. My life for a long time was consumed with my training with Tao Lao and Hosho, trying to understand energy field dynamics. And while I didn't have what you would call a 'normal' childhood, especially after Rani's and my time in the Enchanted World, my area of expertise is field harmonics and specifically how this can speed up the merging of worlds. I know that history is important to some but Rani and I preferred to always focus on the present …"

Matthias felt a cloud of sadness envelop Tan as he spoke of Rani, the woman that he knew Tan had lost shortly after his own wife had died. It was soon after Rani disappeared that Hosho and Tao Lao had assigned Tan to the Peace Embassy on Earth to help Matthias with the integration program.

The Statesman leaned over to comfort Tan patting him gently on the back, encouraging him to share his grief but Tan could say no more. Instead he shook himself, looked up into the older man's electric blue eyes and began to talk of what he knew.

"We did a few classes on galactic history with Hosho many years ago, standard training in dealing with the Volcan Lords. It is written in Akasha, the universal records, that there have been numerous E.T. cultures who have interacted on Earth through time and that some have laid claim to Earth."

"Claim?" Celestia asked, incredulous of the idea.

"Precisely!" echoed Matthias. "But you've heard nothing yet. What you are about to hear my darling, even you will have trouble accepting and you and I are both open, unlike many others. The discussion is then how much of this is to be shared. So, young man, please go on so that we can decide what needs to be told."

~ 6 ~

"Okay," Tan began as they all settled back into their chairs. "Let's keep it brief and to the point. It is said by some that the Orion Grays currently hold economic power on Earth in your time zone and you've known them here via the Volcan Lords. Some say that they are actually adept economic controllers that are pushing to eliminate governments and bring power into the hands of the corporations, which can then control the masses via basic systems of monetary rewards."

"The so-called Illuminati and One World Order groups?" Celestia confirmed then added to her father, "Remember the research you read on all of this just before you first connected with 8tlan?"

"Conspiracy theorists now bore me, sorry but they do. When 8tlan told and then showed me how Universal Law decrees that what we focus on grows, I decided to stop giving any of my time or attention to such things ..." Matthias confessed.

"Wise move," Tan affirmed, "that's what Rani and I also eventually decided. Focus on what we want to create and stop energetically supporting limiting paradigms that no longer serve the whole."

"Isn't that just burying your head in the sand? These things exist so why not acknowledge them?" Celestia asked but Tan was quick to respond.

"Just because something exists in an energy field doesn't mean we want to waste time on it and hence make it grow via our attention. Attention feeds. Chi follows mind – we all know this."

As Tan finished Matthias asked: "I feel the same – so we are agreed. And the Reptoids?"

"Some report that their claim to Earth dates back thousands of years when they began genetic engineering of the Neanderthal stream of man. Sometime after this the scientists from Sirius added their own genetics to evolve Earth's species into the Cro-magnum man, a race that had the ability to mirror their Creator Gods in not just intelligence but also in spiritual awareness ..."

"But if all of this is true, why did this genetic interference occur in the first place?" Celestia asked in a slightly hushed tone fascinated by Tan's sharing.

Tan looked across to where she sat, then breathed out loudly and responded, "Look, when you've been with Hosho and the Light Beings for as long as I have you realize that on one level nothing is true. Everything is just a layer in life, like a movie that is quite illusory in nature yet, like a movie, still runs in select cinemas of belief thus making it true for many."

Matthias sat back in his chair, content to let Celestia talk, as she was always prophetically insightful. Instead she exclaimed: "Well now you've lost me completely. I'm real, you're real, our bodies when we collided earlier in the corridor sure felt real to me ..."

"Have I?" Tan asked softly.

"Have you what?"

"Have I lost you completely? I didn't think that would be possible ..."

She felt that he was teasing her now, almost flirting, as he kept his big blue eyes fixed on hers. He seemed to forget they were in an important meeting. Celestia noted his dark olive skin and thick black hair that he kept braided down his back and felt a slow heat rising up into her face as she sensed Tan's awareness of her changing.

"Seriously Tan just keep it simple would you? I know that life to many is just a dream and that Hosho says 'that the only reality is when we are immersed in the deepest currents of the purest streams of cosmic love, that flow from the heart of creation through the Matrix,' but to others these are just words. To most people everything we feel, see and sense is real, so on this level what do we need to know as Peace Ambassadors for the merging? How do we disseminate this type of information to the masses?"

"I don't think we do," Tan proclaimed softly, looking once more at Matthias. "The Akashic Records tell us that Earth's people were originally seeded by twenty-two different extra-terrestrial races and so on one level your species has the potential to represent the best of it all. Eventually."

"Eventually?" Matthias stated feeling a little more hopeful.

"Eventually," Tan reconfirmed. "Remember your species is still very young in its evolutionary cycle but many hold great hope for you all."

To this Celestia noted, "You talk as if you are no longer one of us."

"I'm not, I guess," Tan admitted, "more of a cosmic wanderer belonging everywhere and nowhere at all."

"Okay, so where were we?" Matthias said breaking the sudden silence between them. He stood up, stretched then sat back down.

"Well," Tan began, "some say that the good news is that the Reptilian genetic line weakens over time and that the original mammalian genetic stream is increasing organically. Others say that the Sirian scientists placed a cellular code, a holographic-type cell within the human stream that would drive human evolution into more peaceful avenues of existence as personal consciousness levels expanded."

"A holographic cell?" Celestia queried, "Tell me more."

"Nothing to tell really. More like as people want to live in peace and enjoy a more harmonious co-existence then the way to do so becomes more obvious to them."

"Like in-built pathways that are revealed by desire?"

"That's it pretty well. Nothing too magical at all. Except that once activated it sets up a path of magnetic attraction to draw the species that are hungry for peace, into peace-filled energy realms," Tan concluded.

"So things tend to take care of themselves once a species reaches a certain level of consciousness," Matthias confirmed of their future.

"The future always takes care of itself, quite beautifully I might add, once we get in the right space in the now moment. And the past? Tao Lao would say 'What was is, and what is, is.' It's what we do now that matters, and how we live each moment as the now determines the future."

"So you're saying that we put the past behind us and do nothing with this data?" Matthias now clarified feeling a sense of ease return.

"We must not lose our focus. We are Ambassadors of Peace, bridges into worlds of peace. Even though the Orion Grays claim to have placed a computer in the subterranean levels of Earth eons ago, that has input energetic pulses through Earth's grid lines to direct Earth's consciousness in ways that serve the hive mentality. Even though they have long held economic control via the Volcan Lords; the Federation of which you are now a Commander has been aware of all of this for eons of time. We are not concerned and we place great faith in the continual development of human consciousness. The Starship Elysium is well positioned, contact has officially been made, the Embassy of Peace has been established and well received and you my friend, are well respected. Yes, I say we say nothing, at least for now. Besides this data is not new for many, key into the World Wide Web and you'll find much more including the tales of the Annunaki."

"But much of what is out there is disinformation, or has been discredited or dare I say sounds ludicrous … our job is to provide positive data that not only uplifts but also educates to create a reality that serves the greater good!" Matthias lamented, so Tan reaffirmed:

"Precisely and so I repeat, we must not lose our focus. Earth belongs to those who dwell upon her now – not to those who seeded her eons ago. Humanity has come a long way and can claim their own sovereign space within the higher realms if they choose and many now have chosen."

Matthias was silent for a while as he digested Tan's words. After a few moments he sighed. "A few years ago I met a warrior Peace Keeper from Orion. Marselan was his name. With him I spoke of many things, the alien abductions on Earth, the fear so many have regarding extraterrestrial Earth invasion. His insights were invaluable …"

"Like?" Celestia queried as it seemed as if her father was now talking to himself.

"Like? Mmmm yes … sorry, I got distracted for a moment recalling it all in my mind … okay, to be brief … he said that all E.T. interaction with humanity happens via pre-agreements made on the inner planes. Often things such as E.T. implants that happen with abductions are just tracking devices and energy healing and balancing devices and that those being tracked are first-borne, star-borne, and well known to the ones who abduct them."

"First-borne? Star-borne? Elaborate please …" Celestia was entranced for she loved these tales and stories.

"Marselan and I were talking about war and peace, how fighting for peace, using violence, seemed so strange to us both. He told me how

Earth is seen as a warlike planet, just as his own system often was. We talked about the policy of non-interference, how E.T.'s can't interfere with a free-will planet like Earth, and how our human species must choose love rather than fear in order to evolve into a more peace-filled direction ..."

Tan could sense Celestia's impatience growing and so he picked up the story, condensing it for a quicker understanding. "There are realms of beings who have never known war or violence, have never felt separate from Source – unlike Earth and those in the Orion and other systems where intergalactic warfare can still be waged. Non-interference is the usual E.T. policy yet it was decided at one point that these pure beings could volunteer to take human form and be a guiding light in Earth's evolution. We call these particular ones first-borne star-borne, for it is their first time on Earth ..."

As Tan paused Celestia asked, "So they come in as babies, through the normal channels? Or as walk-ins or holographic projections?"

"All of those methods but the most common is for their soul to enter Earth's cycle as a human baby."

"Wouldn't they forget who they are and why they chose to come to Earth?" she queried further.

"Some do, many don't ..." Tan responded as Celestia added:

"And if they've never known violence and war, how do they cope with the shock of being in such a dense world like Earth?"

"Imprints," Matthias offered coming back into the conversation again. "Marselan said that in order to handle life on Earth, these souls passed through the Akashic Records where they were imprinted with memories and emotions of other people's lives on Earth, just so that they could cope."

"So if they underwent past life regression therapy, it would seem as if they had lived many lives on Earth when in fact this is their first time?" Celestia was eager for more, her mind moving fast.

"Yes so Marselan said. Tan?"

"What your father is sharing is true. Many have found under deep hypnotherapy, that they are actually related to the various E.T. groups who have been performing the abductions, and that they are on Earth now to spread light, love, compassion, plus awareness of more civilized realms. But yes, many forget this and so memories of abductions – visitations – are often buried or held in a pocket of fear. Still, once those memories are accessed correctly the galactic kin connections and the love the abductors hold for them is evident. All have volunteered to have these experiences but Earth is so dense it is hard for many to remember and stay connected to who they really are and why they have come here ..."

"Okay," Celestia announced as she stood up then headed for the door, "Let's talk more of all this later! I'm tired and also hungry, who's coming to dinner? Father? Tan?"

As Matthias rose to join her Tan found himself thinking that dinner, dessert, some wine and Celestia in his bed was exactly what he was ready for and for the first time in a long time he felt the rising of an inner sense of joy.

Yes he missed Rani, always would, but it was as Matthias had stated, it was time to put the past behind him for what is, is, after all, and right now he was hungry in ways he hadn't been in a long, long time. As for Earth's intergalactic history, he was sure Celestia would soon have endless questions just as he had once.

~ 7 ~

Celestia

Wow, imagine that, was all Celestia could think as she later lay looking up at the stars enjoying the silence and the sense of her own insignificance, that feeling she'd always get with this view. She had taken to sleeping on top of the Embassy roof where her father had created a beautiful garden complete with a place to sleep and a view of a cosmos that never failed to enthrall her.

Billions of stars were blinking in and out of existence, each one sending pulses out into the greater field for others to tune and respond to. Genetic manipulation, galactic warfare, off planet political interference and covert treaties, all of it intrigued her, made her thankful to be following in her father's footsteps. She was born to dance to a different rhythm. Her father may be content to spend most of his time on Earth but she was a cosmic wanderer at heart.

Wow, she thought again as her mind turned to Tan who she'd only recently met. She'd been away, studying on board the Elysium with 8tlan and Tao Lao. She'd envied their love, longed to feel it in her own life, yet had never met anyone of interest until now.

She'd fallen in love with Tao Lao but then all his students did for none were immune to this wise one's charm. Yet whenever 8tlan was around it was plain for all to see, that Tao Lao's heart belonged to only her. It was endearing, reminded her of how her father was with her mother. Adoring, committed, only hers.

Love, everyone is falling in love, she smiled to herself as Tan's face appeared once more in her mind. *Emotion. The emotion of love creates change, drives worlds,* she reflected, remembering what Tao Lao had once said, then wondering what it would be like to feel so secure in someone's love, so cherished and adored.

She never felt much emotion, even before her mother had died and definitely not after. All she felt was numb with her mother's passing, numb at her father's obvious grief and numbed by everyone's kindness.

Tonight it had all changed as Tan's fresh presence elicited things she never knew that she could feel.

She was twenty-eight with five lovers behind her, each one pleasant enough or amusing, but none had touched her heart. Sex? She loved it, loved it more when she'd felt her partner's love and adoration but love her lover fully in return? She wasn't sure she even knew how, so for a while she had been celibate.

"Thought I'd find you here." A strong clear voice rang out to disturb her contemplations.

"Tan," she acknowledged warily, unsure if she was ready to spend more time in his unsettling presence.

"Mind if I join you?" He sauntered over and casually dropped his tall but well developed frame onto the cushions beside her. "Or would you rather be alone?"

"Err … no," she stammered then stood up to quickly regain her composure. Moving cat-like over to the edge of the rooftop, she deftly sat down on the ledge of the small thin rail.

"Not afraid of heights I see." Tan grinned as he motioned to the 30-meter drop.

"Not afraid of anything much at all," she countered defiantly, trying to still her beating heart.

"That's good to note."

Unsure of why he had come and invaded the sanctuary of her space upon the roof, she cleared her throat and queried, "And how can I help you?"

"More like, how can we help each other …?"

"Okay, how can we help each other?"

He would have loved to say to her, *"we could help each other mend our wounded hearts with a little mattress action, right here and now under these stars"* but instead he ignored this sudden desire and asked:

"Apart from your study time on board the Elysium, I assume that this recent journey was your first trip into and out beyond the stars?"

"Yep."

"Loved it?"

"Yep."

"Want to do some more?"

"As soon as possible. How, with whom? When and why?"

A woman of few words, he thought, *gets straight to the point, how unusual.*

"Tan?"

"Ah yes, Congress, Arcturian system, in a month or so. Thought we should go, you can check out their society, gain insight into a truly civilized realm."

"What type of Congress? Are we invited?"

"Not yet but it will be arranged. Big intergalactic gathering, annual convention, a convergence of beings from all the civilized realms – fifth dimensional and above, so 8tlan informs me."

"Do they even keep a body in those realms?"

"Many don't but they do good holographic projections," he responded matter-of-factly, glad she was open to such talk and happy that she had come into his life. It had been a long time since he had even noticed a woman's charms and for the first time in a long time, he realized how lonely he had been. Celestia's mind intrigued him also, just like her defiant spirit.

He had waited for Rani's return for so long, missed her more each day, stayed at their beachside holiday apartment where they'd gone to celebrate their completion of the Heartland Game. And there he had remained, buried under the grief of it all, until Hosho had finally come to lure him back to the Starship.

"Come on young man, enough of this. You'll find her again – one day ..." the wizard had declared but Tan had just looked right through him, then turned and walked away.

A month later Hosho had returned but Tan's reaction was the same.

A week or two after this it was Tao Lao who came.

"We need you," was all his mentor said.

"For what?" Tan had stated with just a touch of anger, resigned now to the fact that they would not leave him alone.

"How much do you know about the assassination attempt that nearly took down the President just before her election?"

"The one that killed Isabella's Yesif?" Tan had asked.

"The same."

"Not much, just what 8tlan had told me, how annoyed she was at you for risking your life like that. Kept saying that if you'd have died, it would have been such a waste ..."

"And Rani?" Tao Lao stated then continued, "How do you think she would feel at you pinning away like this? Wouldn't she say it was also a waste?"

Tan had smiled then, remembering 8tlan's anger at Tao Lao and realizing that yes Rani would feel the same. "Okay, what do you need me for?"

"We need an Emissary, a go-between if you like, to bridge us to the Embassy of Peace on Earth, the one Matthias Inshallah created with Isabella to help with the merging of the worlds after official contact was first made with the Elysium."

And so it had come to pass and here he was now, older, perhaps a little wiser, still nursing a bruised and broken heart but too busy most of the time to notice. For the first time in a long time, a passion had begun to creep back into his soul and her name was Celestia. Dark eyed, dark haired, honey voiced Celestia.

"So," Tan declared as he let go of the past to focus his gaze fully upon her. "We go?"

Celestia's face lit up in a smile. "As long as you promise to tell me more of Earth's intergalactic history?"

"Done," he beamed. "You'll also get an excellent insight of Earth's history at the Congress!"

As Tan and Celestia began to discuss logistics, in another octave of time and light, another couple had begun the dance of remembrance and love.

~ 8 ~

Sarah

Sarah felt high, exhilarated by life as she explored the cliffs and beaches of the island she'd come to call her home. She was pregnant, *eight months now*, the child had telepathically informed her, as they readied her body for birth with the pleasure of food, fresh air and walking. If she was eight months pregnant, she reasoned to herself, then she'd been on the island for at least four months and that meant that a year or more had passed in the outside world.

"Remember," Marselan had said, "one day here is equal to three maybe even four days in your outer world."

"Three days or four?" she asked, "Don't you know exactly?"

"Nah, I've never bothered to venture out into your world. Love my island home, that's enough for me of Earth. Just know our time zone here is slower."

Now every moment that Sarah sat in silent contemplation, the child within her spoke of other lives lived, in other time zones throughout millennia, and that they were both first-borne, star-borne.

"What does this mean?" she later asked Marselan as they sat one evening to watch the setting sun.

The sea was unusually still, had been since her arrival, he had recently told her. In fact everything had been much calmer since she'd come, he'd shyly admitted as he'd leaned in that day to kiss her. It felt good, right, and so she'd kissed him tenderly back. Since then he'd taken to sleeping in her bed, spooning behind her to offer comfort and warmth, to hold her when she needed. He'd also sing to the child that was growing within, as Sarah regained strength but not her memories.

"My child informs me we are both star-borne, first-borne, what does he mean?" she asked again.

"All are star-borne at some time," he casually responded. "Especially on Earth for this planet was seeded a long time ago with genetic material from various sources, other systems of suns and stars," and so he'd told her much the same of what he'd once told Matthias Inshallah in another zone of time.

"And first-borne?"

"It means that this is your first embodiment in this plane of Earth."

"But I have dreams that I have been here for a long time, dreams of other lives ..."

"Imprints," Marselan replied.

"Imprints?"

"It is said that there are many first-borne, star-borne incarnating now on Earth. That these ones are descending from much higher, more civilized realms, realms that have been where Earth is now, realms that have successfully completed their own merging," he paused a moment to let her take this in.

"It is also said that initial adjustments into Earth's field were virtually impossible. To come from such refined planes of existence into a world where war and chaos still reign is too much for these sensitive ones. And so they pass through the Akashic Records and pick up imprints of experiences which allow them greater insights into human nature, insights in the form of cellular memory that is not actually their own ..."

"Cellular memory?" Sarah queried then added, "Mine seems to have shut down!"

He laughed at her attempt at humor, rested his hand on hers. "If it's meant to come back it will. Thankfully we all hold mini video-type recordings of everything we've experienced, within our cellular structure. It's quite easy to access when you know how and if there are things you need to recall."

"If ... that's the big question. Somehow, I don't feel as if I am meant to recall anything from my life before you at all ... anyway let's continue ... can you share more of first-borne, star-borne?"

Marselan paused for another moment unsure how to go on. "We know that all are one in the web of life so none of us are separate and cellular memory is therefore shared by all, still time spent in the Akashic Records allows the descending ones, the star-borne first-life, to assimilate more easily into your world, to be more empathetic. Hence, they also have no past-karma in your world. First-borne star-borne are here to serve the greater good – that is all."

There was so much more he wanted to tell her of exactly where they had both come from and how his life in the Orion system and like her life on Earth, were just two small extensions of the light of the greater beings they both were. Yet he was still tuning himself to all of this remembrance, as if he was gathering small important pieces in a much grander puzzle of life. When he was clearer they would talk. It was enough for him now to know that she had been returned. The fact she came with another man's child was a bonus to them both since exposure to chemical warfare in his youth had probably left him sterile.

Sarah thought of all of this now as she wandered the hilltops, climbing like a mountain goat up to her favorite place. It was a large overhanging rocky outcrop where any loose stone would plummet a hundred meters, before being swallowed up by the waves that crashed upon larger rocks below.

Regardless of her lack of memory, she felt content and strangely whole.

Serve the greater good, Marselan had told her, then added that he'd have to go back to his own planetary system soon. As she continued to climb she knew that wherever he went she would have to follow.

Now and then she'd dream of another time, of a man who mourned for her still, but then she'd wake and feel Marselan's arms around her and the dream would disappear.

Island life suited her. Being with Marselan suited her better still. He told her of his life as an Emissary of Peace who sometimes went to war to defend those who were unable to defend themselves. She had felt the scars that covered his body and knew that each had a story to tell.

And so she sat down upon the rocky outcrop consumed by her thoughts of following this man she'd come to love, who sometimes went to war.

Suddenly a sharp pain pulsed across her belly bringing her back to the present. She massaged her distended stomach then gently began to hum gently to the child within and after a few moments softly said:

"So little one, the sooner you are born, the sooner we can all move on to our next adventure!"

~ 9 ~

Matthias

Commander Matthias Inshallah was restless. The scheme for merging the worlds was just too grand, there were too many factors that needed his time and contemplation, too many fields of possibility that could open and close in the blink of an eye if he didn't stay tuned to the greater game.

He could feel the energy force that was driving it all. Tan called it the Heartland Game, others called it the Field of Infinite Possibilities, while the religious called it the flow of the Holy Spirit.

Matthias glanced up at Tan who sat on the big, soft grey colored couch before him talking to Celestia. They were animated, entrenched as usual, no doubt arguing the finer points of life. They were always like that lately, locked mind to mind as they sought to understand the workings of the fields of life. He assessed them for a moment longer, squinted his eyes, tried to see, then feel the energy flow between them, to sense what was in their hearts.

Celestia's love for Tan was obvious; it shone out of every pore of her being whenever Tan entered the room. She was never good at concealing her emotions and wore her heart on her sleeve. His daughter looked radiant, happier than he could ever recall. It had been a long time since Celestia had displayed emotions at all.

Now she threw her head back and laughed at something Tan said and Matthias felt his breath catch in his throat. In that moment her look and sound was exactly like her mothers. Oh how he missed her still. Every day he spoke to her with all the love in his heart, and in the silent times of the early morning he felt her with him again; an invisible force of love that soothed him in the darkest hours as if she was reaching through the veils from a more angelic place.

Oh my love, Matthias sighed to his wife. *Let us just hope he doesn't break her heart* ... but then his daughter looked up at him and winked as if to respond with her usual confident flair, *"I've got it covered, he's mine, and he just hasn't realized it yet!"*

Matthias smiled then and went back to his work and wondered how Marselan was doing sequestered at his mystical island retreat. *Resting from his war wounds no doubt,* he thought, *bound to be back with the Federation soon, leave him be, he'll make contact when he's ready.*

Marselan. It had been ages since he'd seen him, was amazed at how they'd instantly bonded. Introduced by Tao Lao, Marselan was like the younger brother that Matthias always wished he'd had, a shining light from a war-torn system in Earth's own galaxy. A gentle rogue who fought for the right to be free to choose the path of peace, who'd fight for the rights of others, Marselan was a walking contradiction.

Sometimes Matthias couldn't believe the things he'd been introduced to since the Starship Elysium and its intriguing Commander had arrived. Like many on Earth, he had long accepted there had to be life within the multi-verses but actually meeting with them face to face? That he still couldn't get used to. And the stories both 8tlan and Marselan had told him! Inter-Galactic warfare, struggles for domination of planets and their resources, co-creator Gods seeding many worlds …

Perhaps Tan and Celestia are right, he thought, *perhaps it is time to expand our contacts and walk among those of more civilized worlds.*

"So what do you think Commander?" Tan asked, bringing Matthias back in to the moment.

Unused to his new title Matthias startled then asked: "Think?"

"About our plan?"

"Which one?" Matthias smiled and looked at his daughter again. "You two always seem to have so many."

"The Congress with the Arcturians – we think the Embassy should send a delegation …"

"Delegation? Tan the Embassy consists of only us three … and Isabella who still hasn't rejoined us …"

"And our networks without whom we'd never have gotten so far," Celestia noted. "All of our networks are stable now and all are performing better than expected. Our education programs are in place, all web channels are buzzing and more are tuning in each day," she added then continued: "So Tan and I could go. Couldn't we? You're so deep in the final stages of planning and putting all of our additional projects and programs to paper, so surely you could be without us for a while?"

Matthias looked at them both, put down his pen and listened. He'd never seen either quite so alight before.

"You could come with us, finish the paperwork enroute? Launch the new proposals at the Congress, get some feedback?" Tan offered the elder Statesman.

To Tan, Matthias was far more human than his previous mentors, more approachable somehow, felt like an older brother sometimes, at others like a very wise friend and lately more like a father. "I for one, would love to have you come along."

"Ah ... yeh ... that could work too ..." Celestia reluctantly added.

Matthias could see the excitement fade from his daughter's eyes. He'd be the third wheel if he did come, maybe put a spanner in the works of her seduction plan, so he gently said: "It's a possibility. What exactly did you two have in mind?"

"It's been awhile since you first connected with the Elysium and its crew, hasn't it?" Celestia queried.

Matthias just nodded.

"And since first contact exactly what have we achieved?" she queried.

"With the help of our Cosmic Colleagues I'd say we've achieved a lot ..." her father reflected. "So your point and plan?"

"Is to speed it up," Tan stated simply.

"By attending the Congress?"

"I think we need more exposure to the planetary systems that have been where Earth is today. All systems are confronted during their evolutionary process, by issues such as the use of nuclear power and the need to develop less destructive energy systems, and also how to harmonize the diverse range of cultures etc ... there's also Earth's issue of global warming."

As Tan's voice trailed off, Celestia continued. "I know each system's history is recorded in Akasha where we can now read of it all when we link in via meditation or via Elysium's computer systems, but there's nothing like firsthand experience ..."

"But it would take eons to get there! Isn't the Congress being held 37 light years away in the Bootes Constellation? I couldn't spare you both for so long ..." Matthias proclaimed.

"Already looked at that," Tan said as he jumped up from the couch and came to stand beside him. "Talked to 8tlan, we can take one of their smaller energy field crafts, the ones with I.D. magnetics."

"I.D. magnetics?"

"Interdimensional magnetic attractors," Tan clarified. "They jump the space-time continuum – defy it by repatterning themselves into the Harmonic Resonance of their intended destination. Allows us to travel nearly as fast as we do via the thought process of bilocation yet we get to take our physical bodies along."

"But wouldn't they also repattern everyone inside them?" Matthias was quick to point out.

"Sure but it's not a problem if we stay in the Theta brain wave pattern," Tan assured him.

"Via meditation?"

"You'd need a week or so solid preparation beforehand for fasting and fine-tuning but Celestia and I already know what to do from our training with Hosho, and you're a quick learner so I'm told. There's also the possibility of a group dematerialization and rematerialization but I'm not sure that we are skilled enough yet for that," Tan was now thinking aloud. "But we'll get there quite quickly – one way or another!"

Celestia smiled at her father, her eyes silently pleading for his permission to let them go – preferably on their own but as a trio if he had to come. The idea of time away seeing Tan everyday was making her heart pound. She could not dim the light of hope from her eyes, she didn't want to, as she was finally in love and it felt so good and right. Did Tan love her? Not yet but he would, this was something she knew, like a destiny pre-written.

"And how does the Commander of the Elysium feel about your proposed sojourn to the Congress of these Scientists of Light?"

"8tlan was more than supportive," Tan offered. "Said it's good to mingle with those from worlds who have been where Earth is now, and

who succeeded in harmonization. Also said she'd love to see you again
…"

"And the Elysium always sends their own delegation which we would be part of," Celestia managed to almost breathlessly add, her excitement was palpable. "We'd also love to see them all again … and it seems like forever since I was on the Starship!"

Matthias rose and kissed her lightly on the cheek, "Let me sleep on it. It's a good idea for someone to go I agree …"

"Yes Papa, Tan and me … and … you … of course, if it suits you …"

As Matthias walked the short way back to his quarters, he felt as if he was walking through a tunnel of glass where doorways to parallel realms and future worlds constantly appeared then opened to grab his attention. Sometimes he intuitively knew where each doorway would lead, should he choose to enter, although he had learnt over time not to make rash assumptions for the images each showed were often just one scene in a much grander play.

His choices seemed endless. As 8tlan had once told him, moving an evolving world into a new direction was easy once you understood the workings of the supporting energy fields. By applying the principles of Universal Law and the Higher Light Science, planetary systems could be completely transformed if it was the collective desire of its people. The hard part Matthias now felt, was to not be sidetracked by the myriads of choices and get distracted from the greater game. The even harder part was not acting too soon before all the data had been gathered and sound assessments made. He'd never been rash anyway but now there was Tan and Celestia to consider.

Isabella had been detained in the Middle East working with Tao Lao, assisting him with Peace Treaties and negotiations that seemed to have no end.

"One step forward, two steps back, three steps forward, one step back," Isabella had recently told him when she'd called in her latest Progress Report. "Still at least steps are being taken," she'd laughed with her usual optimism. "Some say there is still a chance of a Third World War and so our work continues! Why is choosing the path of peace over the path of war not the best option?" she had asked but for this he had no answer. He'd thought the path of war had already been so well trodden with dismal results that he couldn't see the point of it anymore. The path of peace seemed obvious, but how? How to change the tide of the habitual nature of man?

Now as he stood under a steaming hot shower Matthias found himself thinking, *When does it all end? Worlds in war, worlds in peace. Civilizations rising, then falling again as people give in to their greed or fail to maintain pure hearted clarity of intention? Sometimes, just sometimes, it is all just too much!* Matthias thought as the water warmed his strong, fit body. *What on earth do I think we can accomplish? Tan, Celestia, Isabella and myself? We are all unusual people but is being unusual enough?*

Dismissing this limited thinking stream Matthias reminded himself, *Step by step, you may not have all the answers but they will come to you as you need them, you know this. Stay present in each moment, stay anchored in the field of love via your daily meditations and just do it step by step* ... and with this he was for now, content.

Space beings, E.T.'s, genetic manipulations, first-borne, star-borne, alien abductions, U.F.O sightings, conspiracy theories ... the list of things to preoccupy them all was vast and so he took a few deep breaths then sat himself down on the shower floor to let the warm streams of water wash it all away. Right here, right now, in the privacy of his shower, Matthias Inshallah relaxed. Yes, right here right now for the first time in a long time, Inshallah let it all go and tried to relax. He was loved and well supported and for now this was enough and as for the rest, he had done all that he could. Perhaps a Congress would be a good place for them all ...

Matthias dreamt of her again that night, that missing piece in his life, the young woman who he'd tried to raise like a daughter but now never saw.

"Godfather," his best friend had asked of him some thirty years before. "If anything were to ever happen to us, we need to know that she'll be yours?"

Matthias remembered the joy alight in his young wife's eyes; felt the ever-present fear that they would never be blessed enough to have their own blood child.

In the dream, he saw the crash again, the car careening around the bend, skidding on the wet road before flying over the cliff. His best friend was burning alive, his body writhing and contorting in pain.

The dream scene shifting to the face of an inconsolable child whose parents would never come to take her home. One night of babysitting turned into a lifetime of worry and concern when the child's mother also failed to return.

In the dream, the endlessly screaming child turned into an endlessly screaming teenager, who seduced too many with her body and her wiles.

The dreamscape suddenly shifted and he saw her slumped over with a needle in her arm, almost lifeless eyes, and cheeks sunken and hollowed, she looked as if she was the walking dead.

Where was she now? he wondered as he woke knowing he had done all he could do when she'd finally disappeared just days before his beloved wife had died. He felt as if he had failed her, and still blamed her just a little for the passing of his wife. "Liver cancer comes from swallowing anger or frustration," he'd once been told and their goddaughter had been the source of both …

They had called her Angel from the moment she'd been born, a colicky restless baby, with big blue eyes that looked into their soul. She was only two when her father had died, just one week before his own Celestia had been born. With a new young baby to care for, a funeral to arrange, and also the disappearance of Angel's mother whose shock at losing her love, had turned her from her child; it had all been overwhelming but they'd done the best they could, hadn't they?

Matthias lay in bed in the early morning light reliving the dream and the nightmare of their life for as Angel had grown, the light had often dimmed from his own wife's eyes. Nothing they did could make their Godchild happy.

Celestia had been easy, a dream child to enjoy, who seemed immune to Angel's anger at the hand that fate had dealt her so soon in life. Obsessed with finding her mother, Angel could never see or feel the love of Matthias or his wife.

"Thank God for Celestia," he sighed in his mind, if it made her happy to go to the Congress, then to the Congress they would go for he felt the need now more than ever to see his daughter's eyes alight with the joy of life. The past was done and the present was all that mattered to him now. And Angel? Celestia was right, she'd come back when she was ready.

~ 10 ~

Sarah

As they sat outside the cottage to enjoy the rising sun Marselan's mood was buoyant. His leg was nearly healed and his heart was full and whole. No longer weary, he was ready to rejoin his crew and Sarah was keen to travel with him.

"The baby's coming early, I sense it," Sarah began. "Yesterday I had what felt to be a contraction, a sharp pain."

"Only one? Nothing since?" he looked a little worried, suddenly aware that they would have to go through the birthing alone.

"Nothing," she smiled then asked, "How long have we left here before we have to go?"

"A month, maybe more, depending on you two," he grinned and patted her distended belly. "Hey little man, no rush, just get here safely, we're new at all this!"

Sarah laughed and then tried to reassure them both. "It will be fine, I can feel it, and we'll know what to do ..."

They lapsed into silence as they often did, comfortable and complete in each other's presence.

"There's a meeting I'd like to attend if you're up to it ... people I need to reconnect with who would be also good for you to meet ... you'd like them Sarah."

"When? Where?"

"A long way from here, another realm, they'll send a small Starship for us if we're ready and the baby has come."

"You've established telepathic contact again?"

"Seems so. It's amazing what being whole of heart can do and the doors that whole heartedness can open. I was beginning to think I'd lost the skill, that too much war and anger had thrown me too far off centre."

Sarah sat for a while in silence then quietly asked, "Could your starship send someone who knows how to safely bring babies into the world, if we need it I mean?"

"Possibly," then noticing her look of concern he added, "I can definitely ask. You're right, it would make both of us feel a little better but how difficult can it be to bring a little one into this world? Women have been doing it since the dawn of time …"

"Well while you find out if we can get birthing help, *if* I need it, I'm going for a long, slow walk. How far to the sacred springs?"

"Just a few miles, it's pretty close to where we were the other day."

"Got it," she affirmed as she rose and kissed the top of his head. "Feel like a day on my own in silence, back by sunset okay? And yes I'll go slowly! Can't walk fast anyway, more like a waddle …"

He'd offered to come with her but accepted her refusal with a smile for the island was now well known to them both and impossible to be lost in.

As Sarah walked, she talked to the son who was wide-awake within her, rolling around gently and stretching out as if trying to make himself more room. The skin on her stomach was stretched so thinly across her, hard and tight to the touch. Strolling along the tree sheltered mountain path, she gently massaged her belly and asked the child to help her.

"Come when you are ready. Come the perfect way that you need to come. Guide me in what to do, I know you can …" she whispered as she walked.

"Yeh come when you're ready. Come the perfect way …" she began to sing.

Sarah stopped for a moment to rest upon a rock that was nestled beside a running stream and the baby readjusted itself within her as a small trickle of warm water was released unnoticed from the pant-less space between her legs. She had no underwear, only her bathing suit plus a few of Marselan's shirts, which she adjusted to fit her as best she could. At night she put on one of his smaller jackets, added a pair of his stretchy pants and socks for feet that were often bare.

She loved the freedom that having so little had brought her, few clothes, few choices, life on the island was idyllically simple.

To Marselan she was beautiful no matter what she wore, still once the baby was born new clothes would be the order of the day, especially for the Congress.

She heard it then in the stillness as she sat at the water's edge. The low soft hum of a distant ancient song that beckoned her to rise and wander on, unaware that the baby had positioned itself even lower within her.

"Come sweet mother," the voices intoned in her mind as she followed the winding stream, stepping lightly over the river rocks that formed a path that was often unseen.

As she looked up to see where the path was leading, a shimmering field of energy formed a doorway before her. Sensing it was the entrance to another realm Sarah continued without a moment's hesitation. She was called and the baby was urging her on.

~ 11 ~

Marselan

Across the valley, night had begun to fall but Sarah hadn't come home. The last of the sun's rays were setting as Marselan strode back into the cottage, grabbed a torch, water, a knife and a blanket and went in search of them both. Instinct told him that the baby was ready to be born.

Marselan moved with grace and conviction, barely noticing his still damaged leg, then strode out of the cottage determined to find her safe and well. He stood for a moment and faced the sinking sun as it cast its multicolored hues across the horizon. Stars slowly woke above him and the full moon was ready to light his way. He said a prayer for guidance, asked the spirit of the land to aid him, then set off along the path that she had taken. Each time a sense of dread began to rise within he quelled it with a deep slow breath and the image of finding her rested and well.

For Marselan, losing her would never be an option, *She couldn't be far from the Sacred Springs, and she must have found somewhere safe,* he told himself over and over but when he got there, Sarah was nowhere to be found.

He lost it then, this strong warrior man who was always so cool in battle. Momentarily defeated, he sunk onto a low flat rock, let his emotions rush through him in turmoil and distress and then began to breathe himself into a more peace-filled rhythm. One breath, two, then three, each one slower than the last, each breath gentle, deep, refined. He felt himself calming, then sent a beam of love from his heart into the surroundings, then projected a violet light beam from his third eye while he gently chanted her name.

"Sarah, beloved, I am here, reveal yourself, lead me to you now." For what seemed like a long, long time, he held this breathing rhythm, as his heart poured out all the love he felt for her to search the dark surrounds.

There was no response.

He couldn't believe it.

Marselan stayed still, became quieter in his mind, and went deeper into that trance-like state of meditation by slowing his breathing further.

He felt drowsy, his leg was throbbing, every cell in his body wanted to rest, then sleep. The night air was cold, the running water from the spring babbling like some demented person. A mosquito buzzed then bit him, and something slimy swam over his feet that were resting in the stream.

He went deeper again, ignoring it all, and felt the purest love flow out from his inner core, then merge into the energy fields around him. All the love he'd felt for her now flowed out from his Being.

"Come," a soft voice soon whispered in his right ear. A small orb lit up before him, then another, then three more. He opened his eyes slowly and saw that they were real.

"Come," they intoned again mind-to-mind.

Making his way further up the stream, Marselan walked in Sarah's footsteps as the five orbs danced to lead the way, and as he walked, he saw exactly what his beloved had seen that day.

Everything had changed as Sarah entered the Sacred Glade where luminescent beings appeared as wise women from another time.

"Welcome, we've been expecting you," the women telepathically offered as they solidified their mist-like Essence, embracing her as she asked:

"The baby?"

"It's coming," was all these gentle ones said.

They led her to a large flat rock that jutted out into a big clear pool. It was bubbling with both energy and warm water. As Sarah lowered herself down, one of the women sat behind her and began to rub her back as they sang, laughed and told stories of this ancient birthing place.

"Women's place," they giggled. *"No men allowed."*

Sarah leaned back and was embraced by someone's arms as another came to massage the moving mass that was now contained in a too tight place. Contractions rippled across her belly, making her wince and cry out as her mind filled with visions. Women had been there in the past, had united in sisterhood, and had shared their pain and joy as each child came into the world.

Comforted by all that she sensed around her, Sarah surrendered into each spasm unable to do anything else. One foot was now in the water as another set of hands began to push the pressure points to ease the pain in her back. Soon more hands stroked her fevered brow as her breath began to pant.

"Good," the wise women intoned, *"nearly ready, nearly done."*

She pushed until she felt she would burst and soon her baby's head began to crown.

"Come," the women sang out to the child as Sarah bore down until its head and left shoulder popped out. As her body rested for a moment between its endless spasms, she felt soft fingers massaging between her legs, gently easing open her vaginal entrance so that the next push would bring the baby fully out.

"A small one," they smiled delightedly.

"No tearing of your flesh," someone else said as they pulled the rest of her son smoothly out, then gasped.

"Born in the caul! Lucky indeed," another noted as they expertly peeled the still intact birth sack from around his form. One last contraction brought the afterbirth out to slide into the water at her feet where it was quickly scooped up and buried. When a tree instantly began to sprout in its place, the women laughed at Sarah's big smile of response.

"Magic place," the women giggled. *"Magic time,"* they said as they handed her back her newly born son. Washed and wrapped in a clean, soft cloth that the women had long ago woven, the baby stared at her as if to say, *"well done and now I'm home!"*

"Blessed ones," the women agreed, pointing to the stars from which these two had obviously once come. Deftly they cleaned her up and as Sarah yawned, she cuddled her new son close then drifted off to sleep still embraced in a wise woman's arms.

Owls hooted. Other birds screeched at the intruder's emergence. It was as if the whole forest had become alive in alarm, determined to alert the sleeping mother and her son. But none of it could stir them.

He saw them resting peacefully in the glen, washed and clean beside a small but potent fire over which a pot of fresh stew was hung.

"Sarah?" he shook her gently and she smiled, stirred but didn't wake. Marselan noticed a movement in his peripheral vision and turned his head as a clear voice sang out in his mind.

"Leave her sleep. Eat and enjoy our Sacred Glade. Women's place only. Except tonight. Tonight we invite you also to stay. Be well, they are yours to care for now."

The trio woke at the light of dawn, their fire still alive and warm yet looking just like a glowing ember. Marselan opened his eyes and saw her staring at him, her radiant face at peace.

"Look," she whispered, "our son ..."

"He's tiny but he'll be strong," Marselan said as tears began to fill his eyes. *Two for the price of one,* he thought as his heart burst with love. *Yes, this boy will be my son!*

"And you my love? Will you?" he added sensing she'd heard his thoughts.

"I am yours already," she smiled aware what he was asking. "Always have been, always will be."

"Always have been, always will be," he softly sighed to echo her words with his own as he leaned in closer to tenderly kiss them both.

And in that moment their bonding was done.

~ 12 ~

Celestia

"All loaded," Celestia sang out in a clear voice filled with glee. She was impatient to get going. "Do you really need all of that?" She pointed at her father's baggage then stopped and apologized. "Sorry, forgot one bag is full of your research and proposals. I am glad you're coming Dad, I truly am. It will do us good, this trip, I can just feel it."

Matthias kissed her on the brow, then buckled in, keen to leave his thoughts of Angel behind. All he had to do was keep busy enough in the day so that he would sleep deep enough at night, for it seemed the nightmares were returning. For three straight nights, he'd dreamed of her then nothing. Always a needle in her arm, always in the dream her eyes seemed dead, devoid of life. Was she a junkie again? She'd been clean for a year before she'd left, a woman consumed with anger ...

"Dad? You okay?" Celestia shook his arm, he had that haunted look again. "You did all you could ... she'll find her way back to us one day ... you'll see ..."

"If only I had your faith in life, my love," he sighed and patted her hand.

"Okay, done, let's go," Tan exclaimed as he took his position at the craft's control panel then glanced quickly at his two companions. "Ready?"

Feeling comforted by his daughter, Matthias gazed in wonder as the craft began to rise straight up into the air. He looked at the Embassy below – an inconspicuous building with state of the art, literally out of this world technology that so few rarely saw.

A handful of people were privy to what they did and the Embassy's connections as they kept their profile low. None had ever seen the sophisticated spacecraft that Tan kept under cover close to Celestia's rooftop garden where he knew she loved to be. She never spoke of Angel unless he did, never mentioned her mother at all yet he knew her feelings ran deep.

Yes, Matthias thought to himself, *attending this Congress is a very good idea.* And with this he relaxed and soon nodded off to sleep.

"Tan ..."

"Celestia ..."

"I was thinking ..."

"About?"

"Well, we have to stop at the Starship Elysium and Dad will be busy with 8tlan fine-tuning the new proposals ..."

"And?"

"Well that gives us time to play."

"Play?"

"Yes, how long since you've been back? Relaxed there with old friends?"

"Not since Rani ..." but then he stopped himself from saying any more.

"Well," she smiled sweetly, "I think you'll find that we have some friends in common."

"Like?" he asked, happy to move their talk along.

"Loki."

"Loki? You've got to be kidding! I didn't realize he was on the Starship when you were there ..."

"Took a position with Hosho a few months before I completed my training and left. He's fun in a big-brother-type way!"

"And Aphrodite?"

"They're there. She and their brand new baby daughter."

Tan's face lit up. "Their daughter? Loki's a father again?"

"Seems so, just heard about it yesterday from a mutual friend on Elysium. Anyway they're good together ..."

"Finally free of the demons of their past ..."

She looked at him quizzically so Tan added, "Long story, tell you one day."

"We've got time, tell me now? Loki never spoke about their past when I was with them and nor did Aphrodite. And what do you mean, Loki's a father again?"

"We can talk about it later, not now. Look!" he exclaimed, pointing to a shooting star, happy to distract her from stories of his past.

Loki's story was his story and Rani's, and they were stories that would prick at his healing heart. He hadn't thought of Rani in days and didn't want to anymore. Finally he could see a sliver of sunlight shining back into his heart. Sunlight was all he was open to feel, at least for now.

And so Celestia watched the passing of the stars as the cosmic sky consumed them. She too was happy to avoid all talk of the ghosts that still haunted her past.

"Warp drive," Tan commanded of the craft, sounding like his favorite old Star Trek Commander. The small vehicle recalibrated itself smoothly to stabilize its inner field and keep its occupants safe then disappeared in the blink of a watchful eye.

Celestia sat in stunned silence as she always did at this point, happy to watch and learn more of the Elysium's systems. Small craft like theirs came and went with surprising regularity as the Starship's inhabitants enjoyed their cosmic wanderer status.

Elysium, she thought wistfully, she'd missed the life onboard her, a life that appealed to the core of her being. Now here she was again, returning, and then soon going further on than she'd ever been.

This time she would be venturing out with those she loved. Oh what a difference a few months in life could make! Back with a father she loved and thanks to Isabella then Tan, she was finally more able to handle life without her mother. And Angel? Well Angel was tougher and smarter than anyone she'd known. Angel would find her way back to them one day, she just had to, that was all Celestia dreamed and knew.

One day the private detective her father had hired would track her down and one day all would be forgiven and she'd come home. Until then, Celestia thought, there was no point giving Angel's life anymore of her time. If only her father would relax and do the same, she sighed as she watched the big man sleeping by her side. His face looked gaunt, his energy field grey and not sparkling with its usual auric light. A tender love welled up within her as she thought of all that they had seen and been through with both Angel and her mother. She was glad he had joined them, they both needed these type of adventures in order to find the brighter side of life. Watching a beloved one die created holes in hearts that only time would mend.

Oh Mama, she sighed inside, *if only you could see us now ...* she let her mind drift again to Angel and wondered where she was. She hadn't dreamt of her in ages, perhaps she was at peace at last, had found her place in the world. She knew her father felt guilty but what was the use of guilt? She'd rather learn from her mistakes and then let it all go and move on ... life was too precious for regret she'd decided once her mother had passed on. And Angel? There was nothing to feel guilty about with Angel. As much as they all loved her Angel had always done exactly as she wanted with no concern for anyone else in life. *She'll be fine,* Celestia had decided, she always was.

~ 13 ~

Elysium

The Elysium shone like a beacon in the night. Grand. Imposing. Calmly sitting surreal-like in a cosmic sky.

Both Tan and Celestia gasped in unison as they saw it now approaching faster than the speed of light. Tan typed in the docking codes required to board, then lent over to awaken Matthias.

"About to dock Commander," he pronounced as Matthias opened one eye.

Within moments connections were synchronized, gangways were laid, doors were opened and warm smiles greeted their arrival.

"Commander 8tlan."

"Ambassador Inshallah."

They melted into each other's arms.

"Good journey?" she whispered to her dearest friend.

"Easier than last time," he laughed so happy to hold her again.

8tlan hugged him tighter, then stepped back and appraised them all before taking Tan into her arms. "You look good," she smiled approvingly, then winked over his shoulder at Celestia. "Time at the Embassy has done you well."

"You too," he grinned, always so happy to see her. "Tao Lao?"

"Busy but back to see me in a day or two and also to attend our meetings."

"Can't stay away from each other," Tan noted.

"Suits us," she grinned as her big green eyes lit up with mischief. "Okay let's get you all settled. Tan, I assume you want your old room? Celestia, there's a cabin next to Tan's – has a connecting door. Matthias why don't I keep you closer to me? There's a visitors berth just a few rooms down from my apartment."

Celestia managed to keep a few paces behind Tan and 8tlan, purposefully pulling her father back and whispering playfully as she did so. "Why father I do believe you have a crush on her."

Matthias blushed, and looked away.

"Don't blame you, she's just gorgeous!"

"Hasn't aged a day, she looks younger then when I first saw her," he whispered back, deciding to play Celestia's game.

"Pity she's in love with Tao Lao," Celestia sighed still grinning from ear to ear at her father's frank admission, "Unattainable, that's why you like her!"

"Could never replace your mum," he said as he squeezed her arm.

"You should, it's time …"

"Yes," Matthias interrupted, "you should, darling daughter of mine. For you it is definitely time and me? Find me one just like the Commander of this Starship and then we'll see."

Two hours later Celestia knocked upon Tan's door.

"Ready?"

"For?"

"Fun and relaxation?"

"Not till I've seen Loki and Aphrodite. Can you wait? You're also welcome to come along …"

"Okay, but give me a quick version of their story before we go? Fill me in briefly while you dress …" she looked at his bare chest and his long wet hair and thought how she'd much rather stay in and play. He caught her look and she sensed a longing mirrored in his eyes, then she shyly skirted around him to sit down upon a big old couch that was scattered with bright cushions.

Tan walked back into his bedroom, threw on a clean shirt, some loafers for his feet then brushed and braided his hair. Where could he begin? How could he fill Celestia in on Loki and Aphrodite's story without talking about Rani?

Returning to his lounge room Tan took a deep breath and sat on a chair where he wouldn't get too distracted. She looked good on his couch but then again so had Rani …

He brushed a stray hair from his face and then began.

"Okay Loki … long time friend … best mate … ragamuffin, mischief-maker. Lost his parents young, took over care of his sister who later overdosed on drugs in Rio de Janeiro leaving two small children behind. Loves Aphrodite, who loves us both and always will … Loki … learns through the school of hard knocks, looks tough, seems uncaring sometimes but is soft as butter inside …"

"Great, got it! And Aphrodite?"

"Childhood friend, entered our lives at puberty, set our hormones raging. Flirt, tantric goddess and a hell of a temptation for most of the men she meets. Pure-hearted, good for Loki but wasn't always so, smart as a whip, cunning, street-wise and sensitive."

"You love her?" she ventured wondering if it was time to talk of Angel.

"Love them both, always have, always will. That enough?"

"For now." She stuck out her hand and he rose up and pulled her from the couch and in one smooth movement Celestia landed gently into his arms. She breathed in his scent and admitted in a husky sigh, "You smell good."

"You do too," he murmured. He was leaning in to kiss her when a loud bang at his open door made them spring apart.

"Loki!" and then he was gone from her without a moment's hesitation.

The noise at the door was deafening as Loki hollered, grabbed Tan roughly into a huge bear hug and like kids again, began to wrestle around.

"Hey bro looking cool!" Loki exclaimed before taking note of Celestia behind him.

"Aphrodite?"

"Coming soon, baby's sleeping."

"A daughter! Loki I can't believe it!"

"Nor can I but it's true and we're good bro, we're all good."

"Back to stay on Elysium?"

"Best place to be, at least for me! Aphrodite's adjusting, misses the beach at Rio … she'll be so pleased to see you … come … we're meeting at our room, then we can go to the bar. Hey you haven't introduced us! Who on earth can this glorious vision be?"

Celestia stepped forward and Tan placed a protective arm around her as her face lit up in the most radiant smile that Loki had ever seen.

"Oh Loki," she laughed, "It's me Celestia! Stop pretending you don't know me!"

"Good God girl so it is – you just look so different! Relaxed, even care-free ..." and then he guessed, Celestia was in love with his oldest friend. "Okay I promised Aphrodite I'd bring you straight to her. Drinks, stories then bed – what do you say old man?"

"Sounds perfect," Celestia and Tan agreed.

~ 14 ~

Celestia

"Oh my God! I can't believe you're back!" Aphrodite exclaimed, rising up out of her baby stupor to show a glimmer of her former self. She was tired these days, always tired, even though the baby had begun to sleep all night.

In seconds Aphrodite had scooped Tan into her arms, holding on as if she would never let him go. Celestia stood to the side taking all of it in. Loki, the God of Mischief, with Aphrodite the Goddess of Love. It was an interesting union to be sure, one that had since born fruit. As Celestia watched them, she wondered what it would be like to lose a child like Aphrodite had done. A son they'd just told her, so they were still grieving when they'd first returned to the Elysium, perhaps it was why they had come.

The air was ablaze with their excitement. Aphrodite continued to lavish her natural charms on Tan who had almost melted away in her arms. It was the most relaxed that she had ever seen him and Celestia was thrilled to see him reveal his softest core. He loved this woman of that she could be sure, just as she knew that he would come to love her one day.

She glanced over to the crib where a peaceful cherub-like baby lay innocent, fast asleep. Celestia blinked back a tear, such was the beauty of the baby girl with the soft blonde curls of her mother, plus her father's long dark lashes and succulent olive skin.

While Aphrodite continued in her exchange with Tan, Loki was adoring Celestia's response to his child.

"She has that affect on us all," Loki whispered in Celestia's ear. "She's going to break a lot of hearts with that face ..." he grinned then shifted his gaze from his daughter to Celestia, "Not bad yourself," he flirted as only Loki could.

Within moments, Aphrodite had released her embrace of Tan, came over to where they stood and grasped Loki by his arm.

"The baby's naming is tomorrow," she glowed as she turned back to face Tan. "Be her Godfather?" then left the question hanging in the air before Loki enthused:

"Sure Tan ... gotta be you ... you're the only one I'd trust with her, you know, should anything happen ... if we weren't around ..."

And Celestia wondered if love could be that cruel that history would repeat itself. *Was this how it had happened with her father and his best friend?* She brushed the thought aside determined to enjoy every moment back on board the Starship without the ghosts of the past.

The night wore on as old friends reminisced and reflected on the fun times times past as only childhood companions can do. The fact that Rani was missing added a poignant note to it all and yet no one spoke of her until much later when Aphrodite kissed Tan goodnight.

"I'm sorry but I don't know how you can stand it. I'd be such a mess without Loki in my life; it was bad enough losing our son! Still ..." she reflected as she glanced over to Celestia, "it's good to know you've begun to move on."

"Have I? You're the only one for my heart Aphrodite," he winked and lightened up the moment.

They rose early in the morning of the baby's naming day, each attending to the details of what had been ordained. While Matthias organized their Congress visit with 8tlan and Tao Lao, Tan busied himself with Elysium's matters of state for they all played crucial roles in the merging of the worlds.

Celestia enjoyed the hour or two that it took her to wander the starships mass; finding that not that much had changed since she had left.

The craft looked like a huge city that sat suspended, spider-like in space. Its central hub was as she remembered, with its elongated corridors and gateways to the Cadet's Training Station, and Hosho's wing of Alchemical Studies with its famous Sacred Chamber.

Spanning out from the core of Elysium was another connecting bridge that led to where the crew and cadets lived and played. Another arm linked into the visitors docking bridge where many new craft were anchored. The final arm that extended from the Elysium's central hub was where the conclaves met and intergalactic business was held.

A bridge connected each nodule, so that they formed an outer circle around the central hub, except for Hosho's chamber, which was linked only to the hub and the training station. The whole thing looked like a spider that was now lopsided by the constant flow of new craft coming to dock for a while, or leaving for their next adventure.

Celestia knew from her first tour of the Starship years before, that when the Elysium prepared for flight the hubs were retracted back into the main body of the ship so that space flight was faster. The exact mechanics eluded her then, and now she had other things in mind.

Celestia moved gracefully along the corridors, familiarizing herself with the small things that had changed and noticing how the feelings she always had there, remained. A deep peace had come over her the moment they had arrived, a sense of purpose, of being part of a much grandeur play. All of this was now mixing in with a subtle excitement of what was to come and how her life would change.

Celestia went to bed that night and dreamt of a son to come who looked like Tan but acted a lot like Loki. As she awoke in the predawn time, she sensed her mother telling her to just enjoy each moment and take one-step at a time.

"And so she will carry the name of Isis," Aphrodite pronounced sweetly as the naming ceremony ended.

"May she be as wise and aware as the one after whom she is named," Loki added.

The baby lay on cushions surrounded by crystals that carried the rainbow spectrum of light.

Tan stepped up to stand beside her and declared, "May the wise ones care for and protect you just as I will always be there in your life."

"And may our lives be blessed by you as we bless you in turn," the trio said in unison speaking ancient words from their hearts. And as she witnessed it all, Celestia silently said the same to the baby of her dreamtime.

Across the galaxy, on an ancient island that was held between the worlds they had known, Sarah stood with Marselan as he held her child up high.

"From the stars he has come and to love's womb of creation he will one day return. We name you now Apollo, for the God of Music, Healing and Light, a God of Truth who could never tell a lie. May you be a Prince of Peace among our ever changing worlds."

Marselan handed the newly named baby back to his mother's arms as Sarah decreed: "Apollo. May all know the music of your light and may all be healed in your presence."

And so another life was blessed and preordained.

~ 15 ~

Days and nights unfolded, as did their endless tales of all that had gone before, and yet no one mentioned Rani again to Tan, nor did Loki speak of his sister Leila or the loss of his first born son and nor did Celestia speak of Angel. Past loves and lessons were destined to stay that way, yet they bubbled beneath their skin only rising to the surface now and then as Loki, Tan and Aphrodite re-bonded just like in earlier days.

Celestia took Rani's place within the group, stepping into their rhythm as if she had always belonged. She brought a different energy to the way they shared, and each day Tan opened up his heart to her and found it strangely healing. Yes, they had all loved and lost but then so had many others. Eventually all hearts healed and finally moved on.

Tao Lao's return to 8tlan and the Starship was also a welcome addition. He brought with him new stories of his work with Isabella in the Middle East where they were forging paths of peace.

In their final meeting Matthias laid out the adjusted proposals for last minute fine-tuning so they could leave for the Convention well informed.

"Okay," 8tlan decreed capturing everyone's attention. "First let's hear from Commander Inshallah, then Tao Lao can fill us in regarding anything else they may need to know for the Congress – Matthias?"

A tall man, Commander Matthias Inshallah unfurled himself from his seat, his blue eyes alive with delight and humor, his heart happy to be with these ones again, happy at the news that he would also soon see Marselan. It was a time of forging both friendships and alliances that worked for them all and served the greater good.

"I've called this 'The Queen's Agenda' ..." Matthias noted then lifted his head up from the plans spread out on the long table before them.

"Good marketing for the mood of the moment," 8tlan observed smiling up at him.

"Yes," Matthias added, "but it's a short term goal. The fact is that we still need to bring the energy field on Earth back into balance, as you long ago suggested."

"We have observed that patriarchal doesn't work as a system, nor does matriarchal," Tao Lao noted.

"True," Matthias agreed. "And so we need a blend. Right now we need more matriarchal energy to bring the old paradigm into a fluid forward motion."

8tlan smiled brightly at him. "Hence The Queen's Agenda, I like it, as I said Matthias, good marketing. I think you are right, many seem to have stagnated in your world. It's almost as if they are stuck in old cycles of habit, unable to see new pathways."

"Celestia and I envisaged a campaign aimed at the women and young adults, basically inviting all to become the Queen or King of course, of their own immediate world. They can all do this by merging more with their Essence to feel more unity and love. From this more enlightened state, we can then shift focus to reprioritize monetary and social objectives and address the last few areas that still bring chaos among Earth's people. Wise Queen's work with compassion; they are tough but fair and merciful. They care but have the courage to change, to meet the needs of the people, to inspire the co-creation of harmony and to do it all with the right blend and variety of attributes.

"Personally I think that those attributes will be crucial keys to implementing the Embassy's full program. There are many women now on Earth who hold positions of power, they seem strong, courageous and to also have a good blend of humility and humor. We also have the multidimensional yet pragmatic Pathways of Peace proposal but I think it still needs simplification so we can reach a wider audience." He sighed, paused then added, "Simple is good, our program needs to be interesting, educational, yet brief and to the point; easy to apply, a system that works quickly and well."

The meeting flowed on as Matthias answered a myriad of questions until his plans had been thoroughly discussed and fine-tuned.

8tlan was glowing, pleased at the Embassy's proposal, it was exactly what was still required. She sensed that Matthias would present it well at the upcoming Congress. It was clear adjustments still needed to be made when they released it back on Earth, but as a proposition at the Congress, it would all present well and hold everyone's attention.

Satisfied she turned to face Tao Lao, "Welcome back …"

"Commander 8tlan," Tao Lao acknowledged formally as he gracefully rose from his chair.

"Before you pass on any advice to the team regarding their trip to the Congress, you spoke recently about India?" 8tlan queried.

"India," he reaffirmed.

"We take it that your work is now nearly complete in the Middle East and so India calls?"

"Once the baseline program is in place there's little else we can do in the Middle East but wait and let things flow, so yes it's time to move on and yes, India calls …"

"Baseline programs?" Matthias interjected as he readied to take notes on insights of interest. Tao Lao always had great ideas.

The monk's brown eyes were dancing as he spoke about how both personal and global energy fields were always run by the will and clear intention of the people and not their governments, and how harmony was easily achieved when the field dynamics were understood and certain programs were applied.

"First step, everyone agrees on the intended outcome," Tao Lao stated.

"Time for harmony and peace," Tan offered.

"Plus agreement creates unity," Tao Lao smiled. "Next step, education into the benefits of applying Universal Law and the Baseline Essence Program Codes with its Triple Win Program, and everything should run by itself …" as Tao Lao summed it all up in the most matter-of-fact fashion, he noted Celestia's curious expression then elaborated as if to remind her, "The Triple Win code? You've all been trained in this aboard Elysium … the one that brings through perfect resolution to all areas of conflict in a way that benefits all? Good baseline programming can shift the direction of evolution of any world …"

"Specific programs like?" Matthias interjected.

"Well, for example the 'Perfect harmony, all fields now', code said with sincere hearted intention. When enough people command this, then the quantum field begins to respond and download triple win solutions where appropriate so that harmony can rule.

"Another good program we use Matthias, is 'everything about my Being enhances this world and everything about this world enhances my Beingness'. For this to be a truth the evolving species will be magnetized out of the dual natured reality plane and into the plane of harmony, mutual enhancement and Oneness.

"We have others of course that I am happy to provide you with …" Tao Lao smiled at Matthias, then added, "of course they must be heartfelt and also said sincerely by enough for real changes to begin. That's one of the problems still in the Middle East, we have the coding locked in but not enough support yet for mutual enhancement games. The balance of power there is still undergoing great change … to some a Third World War is still a possibility, although one that few care to focus upon!"

Celestia nodded then asked, "So can the predicted Third World War be averted there? And now that you have done the basic fieldwork for the Middle East, where does India fit in? Does this mean that Isabella will not be back with us for a while?"

"Not if you can spare her. Again if you look at the 2012 timeline there's something magical being reborn in India that is sweeping through Earth's field." Tao Lao wistfully offered, "Maybe it's just a reclamation of all they already know. Even though the energy of the Rainbow Serpent is now focused on the Andes in South America still it feels to many that India is being reborn, that India's people have a huge gift for the new world. So Isabella will simply tune in and watch what is happening there for a while, at least until after the Congress. We can all meet at the Embassy then. What time do you leave us in the morning?"

"They will depart from the Sacred Chamber at dawn," 8tlan responded. "Do you think to join them?"

"Perhaps …" Tao Lao smiled, "we could discuss this later tonight?"

As the meeting came to a natural close with new agendas born, Matthias realized he was ready to leave for the Congress was calling and a new future was dawning for them all.

Everything was aligned on Earth, yet they were only as strong as their weakest link and some on Earth had yet to tune in and listen, then rise to their own heart's call. And this they all knew, would occur when the time was right, just like a flower that would eventually blossom in its own time within a garden of fertile soil. Still Matthias thought, he'd add Tao Lao's baseline programming codes to the Embassy's agenda for without good soil many flowers could not blossom.

Matthias noted how Tao Lao had skillfully avoided answering Celestia's question about the prophesized Third World War. Could this be averted? Was it all really as simple as the adaption of Universal Law?

Matthias had tried so hard not to get bogged down in the games of chaos on Earth while still remaining well informed. He knew that like attracted like, that it was crucial to use their creative power wisely, to dream then create that which was for the highest good of all. But sometimes, the task before him seemed so overwhelming. Still every moment was new and every choice brought a chance for a fresh beginning.

If only he'd known all of this when he'd agreed to raise Angel, he thought, as he prepared for sleep that night. Would she come again in his dreams, was she finally reaching out and if so what was she trying to tell him?

8tlan had sensed his sorrow deep within and had agreed to help him if she could. Maybe she could sense where Angel was and help to bring her home ... Maybe Celestia was right, the past was done and Angel would return whenever the time seemed right? And if she didn't, or couldn't return? Matthias shook his head and decided to just enjoy what lay before him and let go of the ghosts of his past for the game of "what if?" only brought him sorrow where Angel was concerned.

~ 16 ~

Matthias

The team sat in deep meditation, ready to begin raising their personal frequencies to the octave that would allow a quick transit through the realms and into the Arcturian system. None of their available craft could enter the dimension into which they were bound but no craft was needed. Many spaceships were just a formation of thought that acted as a shield around the inhabitants. Composed of the blended energy fields of its occupants most starships were maneuvered by thought or crystalline power. In the denser dimensions the craft acted as a buffer so that the refined energy patterns of those inside were protected as often the energy flows in the denser realms were too toxic for these ones. Where they were going now, there was no need for such protection for in these higher realms all knew and loved the Source of life within.

Instead they sat together in Hosho's Sacred Chamber, holding hands to unify their energy fields and distribute the power. Here those trained could aid Celestia and Matthias to hold the required brain wave state to dematerialize with the team.

Matthias felt alive, young, energized by the group as a flow of high pitched, deeply pleasing sounds and tones permeated the chamber. The walls were made of crystals that began to pulse with rainbow light, as ancient chants joined the new tones that some of the group were making.

The cells in his body began to hum and vibrate as huge waves of circular energy coarsed through him, flowing up his spine and out through his crown. It then encapsulated the others in its field before flowing back down into the floor. Entering his body again through his perineum, the energy rushed fluidly up his back to fill his spinal column with a tingling bright white light.

He sensed a Torus shaped energy pattern appearing around the group then felt as if he was beginning to dissolve, so he tried to let go of all thoughts. Instead he relaxed deeper into a wave of love that now rose with a spiraling flow of light that felt comforting and familiar.

The group unified as one mind and one heart pulse – each one vibrating at higher and higher tones of color, sound and light as they visualized their intended destination.

Matthias felt the room disappear, then floated out of his body to drift like a stream of cosmic dust across a star-filled sky, trusting that a trail of his body molecules were following close behind.

Suddenly there was new sensations of sounds and lights as he felt hands solidifying in hands as the group began to appear and take a more solid form.

Matthias was awestruck, unable to believe what had occurred for they'd just transmigrated billions of kilometers within the blink of an eye.

The group were quickly engulfed in a pulsing field of light that seemed to irradiate their systems as well as ground and stabilize them. Matthias felt giddy, nauseous. He took a few deep breaths and began to pat his body all over as if to check if everything was back in place.

"Wow, we're all here, even our luggage has been beamed in! You two okay?" he checked with Tan and Celestia.

Celestia nodded as the group found themselves surrounded by shimmering fields of light that solidified to take form. Tall beings, short beings, big blue eyes, small black eyes, bluish skin, whiter skin, golden skin, the beings now around them were of many variations. His daughter was excited, so was he.

They took a few deep breaths then held out their hands to say hello. Instead, the ones around them beamed out rays of the warmest flow of love that entered their hearts which responded back in like. Matthias found himself wishing that people could do this on Earth, for it was an energy exchange of pure love and acceptance.

What a ride and what a welcome, he mused as the group were guided to their apartments.

~ 17 ~

Mary

Across the universe in a dimmer dimension of light, all that needed to be done, had been, and the fields were aligning much quicker than many had expected.

Enjoying a quieter life, Mary had tuned herself to the fields of dance and music, aligning herself to the angel's way, where she found their tones were just waiting to flow through her.

She had asked to harmonize her Beingness on all levels and then applied some other programs that she knew would make life zing a little more. Everything was aligned and clicking in, she felt like she stood on a rock so solid and well supported, and that she'd never felt so blessed and nor had she ever been so ready.

Mary turned to Jacob, facing him fully as she began her daily dance to weave the new rhythms that were flowing through her with their tones to enhance the Matrix.

He'd sensed it too she knew, maybe not as strongly as she did, but he felt the Grace, saw the delivery of something new being birthed on Earth from the void. He knew the seeds had long been planted and that all was growing now, entangled and pulsing with life.

Mary was right, Jacob thought as he lay on their bed watching her dance, they'd needed the break, needed it all. *It was so obvious, yes, seeds and dreams do come into being.*

Their years in Europe seemed like another life, lived by other people than who they had since become. Moving to Australia, buying the old farmhouse, watching each other relax back into a more natural rhythm of life, all of it had been so good for them. Their only concern had been for Rani who Mary sensed would yet return.

She was stretching now, opening her system to receive a stronger voltage of cosmic forces by aligning in deeper, purer ways. As she danced she thought of Tan and his new girl. Mary liked her, Celestia was feisty. Matthias Inshallah had done well, single father, mother passed over, they were both switched on and focused. Father and daughter, both were bright and both enhanced the other.

Connecting in telepathically with Tan, Mary exchanged her *"hello's"* and *"how are you's"*, listened, then shared, and then came back in her mind to the room where Jacob still lay on the bed enjoying his own private rhythms.

She loved the way that she could come in and out of her body like this, sending a part of herself out to tune into different fields of other being's creations. People's personal movies of creation were everywhere dotted throughout the Matrix. Their energy membranes, their energy pulses, their creations, all of it melded into the most amazing tapestry of divine expression that Mary had ever seen. She had time now to look at creation more closely and to influence the flows in a quiet gentle way.

"All is good," she smiled at Jacob, "with them, I mean," she added referring to Tan and his group.

"Are they still on board the Elysium?"

"Just leaving," Mary sighed.

"They'll be fine," he reassured her. "Tao Lao does this glide-through-the-interdimensional-doorways game all the time. Or are you thinking of Rani?"

Mary was silent then smiled. "I know she's out there somewhere but I miss her and yes I do wish Rani was going ... I know Tan hopes she's still alive and I also sense she is ... I know she comes to me as I dream but I never remember our sharing. I guess I just wish they'd find each other again ..."

Jacob motioned to her and she came to lay by his side. "She'll come back to us one day, when the time is right," he offered gently as they lay together enfolded in loving arms.

Rainbows had found their way into Mary and Rani's dreaming where Rani was Sarah as well.

In life and in the dreaming Rani as Sarah was in a deeply contented space. For her, Marselan was an excellent mate – attentive, kind, a passionate lover who had once been in her past. Reunited with this one, she felt as if her heart had once more found a home. His love was all around her, he infused her with his touch and in this her heart was still. Their bodies remembered all their past lives shared and in this field, they played. And in the dreaming Rani would often meet with Mary as she did again that night.

"It's enough for now," Mary had smiled at Rani in the dreaming undeterred that this was the only way they could meet. "I'm just so happy to find you again."

"He calls me Sarah, and that's who I am when he's near. With him I feel so ..."

"Complete?" her mother offered, assessing Rani as they both flowed deeper into the dreamtime plane.

Rani nodded and then stepped forward to hug Mary again. "Yes," she whispered to her mother, "With him I feel like I've come home!"

Mary and Tan, Rani thought, her life had once been always filled with Mary and Tan.

"How is he?" Rani had asked her mother one time when they'd first met in the dreaming plane.

"Better."

"Tell me more ..."

"Tan works too much, I'm sure. But Matthias Inshallah has a daughter, Celestia, she's smart enough and pretty enough to challenge and distract him from time to time."

"They work together with the Ambassador?" Rani queried further, trying to put faces to the names that she heard. "Did I ever meet her?"

"No my love, she came to him more recently, long after you disappeared."

"They are bonding?" Rani had to ask for not too long ago Tan had held a sacred space within her heart.

"Bonding? Perhaps. He still mourns for you my daughter, this is plain to see."

"You've told him of our meetings in the dreamtime field?"

"Yes although I tend to remember so little. Has he not yet come to you in dreams himself?"

"Perhaps we enter the dreaming at different times," Rani sighed then added feeling more like Sarah, "sometimes it is good to leave the past to the past. Marselan and our son is all I wish to focus on for a while ..."

They'd faded then, moving away from each other's channels to awake in different worlds.

~ 18 ~

8tlan

While Mary enjoyed her time with Jacob, the Starship Elysium continued with its vigil in Earth's skies. Anchored behind the North Star, 8tlan was happy with their progress and that Tao Lao had decided to join Matthias at the Congress. As she sat in the stillness of her usual evening meditations, she noted that there were new rhythms flowing through the Matrix all the time as different beings moved their own movies of reality to other levels. She knew that all human life-waves did this, that there would always come a time for them all, where they would be more open to new ways of evolving. Humans struggled, she knew, until the technological advancements came, and then the understanding of how to use them wisely. And with all of this came the insights to learn to curb their destructive nature.

That was part of her job, and had been for a long time, to watch the risings of the worlds and assist when each call came.

As all life was held in the deepest currents of rhythms of love that when explored they became lost in, in a way that made them feel part of a whole and no longer separate from Source, whatever they dreamed the Source to be. To some Source was God, to others a white hole, the centre of origin of the Matrix.

8tlan knew that many were bathing in these energy fields now, not through rules or requirements but just through their own inner calling, because of the nourishment that these new energy fields contained.

These rhythms of love had always been the base frequency in the Matrix. 8tlan had watched so many civilizations grow and develop from that base; aware of it, fully loving it and in tune with it, only to then slowly lose contact with their Source as their own creations entranced them.

While all beings were programmed to be gods in form, to share the same software programs as the original fields of intelligence that ran the Matrix; many forgot this over time and so they suffered greatly which in turn gave them character and depth.

The rhythm of love was the dominant pulse that they had all learnt to tune in to, the pulse of divine wisdom, which came not as a wave like love, but instead as a ray of light. It held within it everything they required to create well and wisely, to enhance the Matrix further, to make it blossom like a lotus flower that reveals itself to the morning sun. This was what Hosho and Elysium life had taught them. Beauty was everywhere in the Matrix. Remembering this, seeking to see it, to know it, to express it, had become another part of their natural way of Beingness.

To 8tlan it was simple. To those attending the Congress it was understood. But to the majority of those on Earth? Well 8tlan knew that this depended on what timeline she tuned into for in her realm, life ran in simultaneous patterns of energy whereas on Earth most saw it still as linear.

Right now, Tao Lao and Isabella were fixated on the year 2012, stimulating and inspiring those in positions of power to make the necessary commitments to negate the still small possibility of another World War.

Yet all around them parallel realities flowed like tributaries of a big river that was Earth's main evolutionary flow. All of it was worth watching and all of it could be changed. 8tlan took a big breath withdrawing from her contemplations on the Matrix as the face of Matthias flowed into her mind.

She'd sensed his sadness as he'd shared of his recent dreaming and his life with Angel through her teenage years. He'd told her how Angel had screamed at him that it wasn't her fault that his precious wife was sick, that at least Celestia had a mother who'd stayed and then she'd left with a slam of the door behind her.

He assumed she had gone to find her mother again, chasing another lead but that had been years ago now. Before she'd always returned to him, a few weeks on the street searching, always searching but she'd never stayed away so long and then there were the dreams … perhaps 8tlan could help?

8tlan hugged him then and he'd stayed in her embrace, feeling the comfort that can come in a true friend's arms.

"I'll do what I can," she'd whispered as he regrouped himself enough to get back to his chamber and sleep. She'd never seen him look so sad.

Therefore, she settled back into meditation and scanned the lines of time around the Earth, weaving her way through the Tapestry of Creations that seemed to be so real.

In a parallel life, 8tlan found his Angel healthy with her parents alive and in love at her side, for Angel had dreamed this reality into being every night. In another flow Angel sat beside Matthias and his wife, a smiling toddler at her side, again in this life, they were all healthy, happy and alive and 8tlan knew that Matthias had dreamed this parallel life into being.

Each existed in the fields as all lives do when the dreamers long for it with passion. And so 8tlan continued to scan throughout Earth's fields, looking for his Angel.

The tapestry was complex for there were not just parallel realities but also future fields of possibilities that were waiting to be set. In one of these flows, 8tlan saw Matthias who now stood at the side of his Angel's hospital bed, his eyes filled with sorrow and compassion.

8tlan watched it all unfold on the inner plane where she could see and feel the flows of the fields. She tuned in deeper to the one that Matthias had called daughter, a wise angelic being bound to Earth, one whose wings were clipped with time until she could fly no more.

So much potential, so many doors his Angel had opened to explore, living her life to the fullest, cramming into her days the dalliance of heightened sensory delight. To some she was strong and courageous, a warrior of a woman hell-bent on having it all, yet to 8tlan she was complex and somehow incomplete. A sweet adoring child, used to having her way, batting her big blue eyes and using her charm to score, yet tenderhearted, sensitive, with so many choices always offering her more.

8tlan watched it all, transfixed, trying to sense the timeline date of what was now unfolding. Matthias had said he had seen his Angel in his dreams, a needle in her arm. Was this scene she now viewed really

Angel's future? And if so, was the vision before her something to share with Matthias?

~ 19 ~

Sarah

As 8tlan worked her way through the myriad of creations within and around the Earth plane, hoping to help Matthias find his Angel before the future she had seen could happen, Sarah was trying not to feel too overwhelmed by her own recent travels.

"This way please," the young woman gestured to her group who were now being ushered into the largest open-air auditorium that Sarah had ever seen. It felt familiar with a touch of déjà vu. She settled in beside Marselan then let her mind go to her boy in the children's zone, only to sense him asleep dreaming of their Avalon Island.

The journey had been strange. Again, she could not shake the familiar feeling that she had done it all before, been somewhere similar. Not with Marselan, not with their child, but in another time, a life when she was younger, on her own.

She relaxed, let the past go, opened to what was there, felt Marselan become fluid and still beside her. She sensed energy tendrils of mental exploration flowing out from his mind and heart as he allowed his conscious awareness to expand and feel then know the surrounding crowd.

Tens of thousands had been called, and now most in the auditorium were doing the same, adjusting their energy radiations to blend, merge, sense and see.

"Rani," Sarah said to herself in a whisper as she remembered a small part of a recent dream where she had met with a loved one called Mary. "I'm Rani."

"Mmmm?" Marselan opened his eyes sensing the change in the one he loved beside him.

"Rani," Sarah said again, "that's who I was before you found me …"

"Nice," he smiled, "suits you," then fell back into silence for a while. She would talk when she was ready; he knew that of her now.

"Well, this Rani I was can stay in the past, I like who I am now!" was all she said as she closed her eyes to blend herself with the energy rivers that pulsed throughout the crowd.

Slowly Sarah relaxed for their initial journey to the Congress had been intense. One moment they had been on the small hilltop overlooking the beach, with their few belongings strapped onto them and the baby in her arms, then as Marselan's arms went around them both, she'd sensed the craft appear then hover directly above them.

A brightly lit star-filled sky, no clouds, a full moon shimmering across the ocean ... that was all she saw as light pulsed through them along with sonic rays that seemed to be disassembling then rearranging their molecular structure. Then just as quickly, their bodies reformed themselves to leave them feeling lighter as they stood aboard the craft.

"Marselan?"

"*Here.*"

"*I can't see you, can't hear anything, yet I can sense everything in my mind. We're telepathic?*"

"*Yep. Easier.*"

"*I remember ...* " she relaxed a little more as the light began to fade to a brightness that was not so overwhelming.

"Are we all amped up?" Marselan asked the crew who appeared around them with their entry to the craft.

"As much as their physical system can tolerate right now," a voice responded nodding to Sarah and their baby.

"We had to adjust the flows for the child," another added.

They were still just voices to Sarah, blobs of color with sound. Her head felt light yet clear, empty yet knowing at the same time, as if she had been rewoven into a vast web of light.

"Wow! Some ride ..." she whispered to herself, and then checked on the baby.

"Fast asleep as you can see," the captain of the craft noted, winked at her then smiled up at Marselan. He had never thought the old warhorse would ever settle down yet here they were - the Commander well healed, his heart alight with love, plus the woman who had transformed him.

"Time to go, everyone ready?"

And that was that, in another blink of the eye they had left Earth long behind, travelled through various portals of light and arrived.

Focused back in the auditorium Sarah took a few deep breaths then opened her eyes and drank in the view of a changing cosmos above them. The Congress hall was roofless yet via her inner vision, she knew it was encased in a flow of circular energy waves.

"Sense anything else about your life before I so luckily found you my Rani?" Marselan poked her gently in the ribs to make her relax and laugh.

"Sarah, to you, just Sarah, and no, nothing yet, but I've a feeling this place and being here with everyone, may just bring it back. If and when it comes, you'll be the first to know ..." she leaned over and kissed his cheek just as the MC appeared.

"Welcome! Welcome delegates, welcome!"

Later that night Sarah tossed and turned, her dreams invaded by a tall dark young man who knew too well who she was, who kissed and held her as they talked for many hours. While her dreams were forgotten in the waking hours, the next day as she walked the halls of the Congress it was almost as if she was waiting for a meeting to occur. She sensed that she had liked the life that she had once known, although she liked her new life even more. To Sarah it was as if she had been Marselan's mate forever, so did the past really matter when her life now was just so right?

~ 20 ~

Celestia

"Ready? Tan are you ready? Come on, let's go!" Celestia was knocking on his door, her energy impatiently bubbling. They had managed to catch a few hours sleep, having roamed the facilities for hours the night before and now she was hungry. Still half-asleep Tan slowly came to open the door and let her in.

"I'm going to meet everyone in the breakfast area, shall I wait for you or go on ahead?" As much as she would have loved to wait and watch him dress, there was a new star-system to discover, unusual people to meet and encounters to be had and she was energized as never before!

"Go ahead," Tan, laughed sensing the wild urge she had to explore. Celestia rose up on her toes and kissed the tip of his nose then lightly brushed his lips with her own.

"See you soon!"

For a moment she had looked just like Rani, Tan thought as he tumbled back into his bed. It was 5am back on Earth and too early for anyone but the birds, but God she had looked good. Perhaps the next time she kissed him they would both be back in his bed and definitely not sleeping.

Now the spotlight was on them. Commander Matthias Inshallah stood tall in front of Tan and Celestia who had remained quietly in the background while he took the stage.

"Embassy of Peace – Earth Delegation," he proudly announced.

Suddenly there was a buzz in the air, a feeling of poignant expectation, so strong that it was palpable. The crowd became silent as Matthias bowed before them and began to share of their life on Earth. The audience was spellbound, waiting for their chance to ask him questions. The experiment that Earth was undergoing was coming to completion and this time it finally looked successful. Yes, the spotlight was definitely on Earth and her people right now.

Celestia found it fascinating, with every speaker the heavens above them shifted like the Star-walk program on her computer, to light up the star-system where each of the delegates was from.

The representations of the day before had been vast indeed and her mind had been well expanded especially with the first speakers who had come in from Orion and later that night she had gone with her father to see his old friend Marselan. They had met at a bar that had served the most intoxicating fruit cocktails that had sent her taste buds to heaven. She soon left the two old friends to talk, to wander off and see what Tan was doing and the night had been fun as they had explored the city together.

She was happy, her father was happy and now he stood upon the stage.

Celestia refocused back on the moment, leaving the memories of her night with Tan behind her. She looked at his long lanky frame beside her, it was just muscular enough to set her heart racing yet it was more than this that had grabbed her, it was what his frame contained.

She shook her head to concentrate again, on what her father was sharing. His audience was spellbound. To Celestia, it did not make sense. What the other delegates had shared had often been far more entertaining yet not once in the past few days had any audience been so attentive.

Why Earth? she thought, *what was transfixing them with what her father had to share?*

As Matthias continued to speak, she watched the cosmic skies above him change as the Milky Way and then their Solar System came into clearer view to focus on the beautiful blue planet called Earth.

It was as if the scenes were revealing a linear snapshot in time that was reinforced by a flow of data across the skies, to support what Matthias was sharing.

The presentation truly was impressive as another layer was added to his view.

"So let's look at the Earth time-line of 2012, this is the one that I am told is destined to have the greatest impact in the Universal flows," and as he spoke the data lit up in the sky above him.

Earth – 7 billion humans and growing.

Earth – long known as a planet of war-like people.

Earth – one of the few planetary systems whose people have forgotten who they truly are.

Earth – scheduled to complete the rising as soon as the majority desired the paradigm of peace to be a reality and not just a dream of potential.

Earth – recalibrating itself more into the rhythm of health and harmony.

Earth – splitting itself like two halves of a pair – one consumed with love and one consumed with fear.

Earth – where political systems were crumbling as people discover the master within and no longer look to others to lead them.

Earth – where greed driven economies were changing, as new ways of providing and sharing resources were beginning to be born.

Earth – transitioning from the third dimension, out of the linear time zone of the fourth dimension, into fifth dimensional simultaneous time expression.

Earth – with its cosmic interdimensional connections.

Earth – long held in a tractor beam of loving support of higher dimensional Beings of Light.

Earth – holding the Shamballa template and destined to know peace.

Earth – with all life forms originally seeded from the higher dimensions.

Earth – current home to a vast array of ET intelligence who has chosen to be born as humans.

Earth – with its first-born star-borne influx arriving after World War II.

Earth – ET immigration status – around 20% of the current 7 billion population.

Earth – with its ET immigrants spread out wherever was needed through all fields of influence; education, science, arts and agriculture - with many also focused on creating alternate energy systems for self-sustainability and better resource usage.

Matthias had paused for a moment while the cosmic screens showed what other ET groups were doing on Earth, then went on.

"So as we were sharing, nearly sixty ET races have had contact on Earth with those in a position to help the populace.

"Contact has occurred from both ET's and Beings of Light with various governments and also with those open in the general population.

"Usually the E.T.'s are in human bodies that have been encoded to hear the call. We have also observed that the ET nature, that is deep within all humans, is currently being activated into higher levels ..."

Celestia noted that this was due to Earth's entry into the Photon energy zone, which was cyclical in nature as Earth passed through it every 26,000 years. The Congress members had also witnessed that contact with photon energy definitely improved a planet's evolution.

Matthias continued, "Photon energy, also called chi or prana, is now known on Earth to improve the rhythms of health, happiness and harmony within all who align their systems more to these energy streams."

Celestia could see this clearly by the images that were flowing now in the sky above the auditorium, where a huge hologram of planet Earth had now appeared. From this perspective, Mother Earth was glorious and she was awed by its beauty. They could all sense the wonder of her spirit being which was so engrossed in its own transitioning, as sparks ignited volcanically, and waves of energy reverberated continually within and around her. Gaia's spirit was unfolding like a hibernating bear, stretching, unfurling, and expanding herself in the cosmic sky above them. Yes from this perspective, it was clear that Earth's spirit was alive and rising, blossoming like a flower. Even Matthias had stopped talking, as the sight had mesmerized them all.

Next, they saw waves of energy rebounding out from Gaia's heart core, waves that travelled out multidimensionally to open more inner plane doors. Key-codes had been ignited and heart-calls had been answered for people's hearts had turned to peace.

The Torus pattern was then revealed as it worked its delicate science to lift Earth into a higher zone. People's membranes were meeting and merging, being repatterned by their thoughts and by hearts filled with compassion and care. All could now see Earth's movement in the tapestry of life, but more than this, … the whole universe was coming along for the ride as if to support Earth's birth into a higher plane of light.

Celestia witnessed this science of the rising, overwhelmed by what she now saw. A part of her couldn't wait to later meet up with Tan and discuss it all in depth but the scenes were shifting as they drew her eyes in deeper through the delicate streams of the Earth's Torus energy field.

There she could see bodies moving, being pulled by different tides, there she could see each person's membranes and the way they met to glide into or collide with each other, always growing and later moving on. It was like a dance, a waltz of movement where sometimes explosions occurred as ego driven games collided with their own power and might. She observed how other rivers of energy and membranes transitioned peacefully to harmonize all that they touched.

The game was completely enchanting and what Celestia really loved, was that the Torus pattern was part of the driving mechanics behind it all. She had never seen this powerful pattern so clearly before or the mechanics of a higher science displayed in such a manner.

"So," Commander Matthias Inshallah concluded, "we have all been busy and we thank you for your support! We are aware of the interdimensional agreement of non-intervention, unless called and thankfully, Earth's call has been well answered! Evidence is mounting as we have just seen, that Earth's presence in the Tapestry of Creation is becoming much more clean."

Matthias continued effortlessly as if he were addressing old, dear friends, "The plan for all of you, to send your representatives among us – via being back in a human body, or doing more holographic extensions – all of this is aiding this 2012 timeline shift as we continue to collectively hold the paradigm of peace in our hearts. At the Embassy, we will continue to simplify our programs so we can educate more and thus create a smoother transformation. And so the dance goes on!" He bowed to his audience then and fell silent.

The response was overwhelming as beings whistled and cheered.

~ 21 ~

"This has never been done before!" someone stated loudly with excitement. "I've certainly never seen the rising of not just a planet and her people but also the whole universe! How amazing!"

"Yes, well done!" others agreed.

People chatted and twittered like birds Celestia thought, then three tones rang out, high octaves that changed the field of light above them.

Celestia saw the scene unfolding like a telescope drawing out, as Earth and its patterns and people became smaller. Soon Earth sat still, a small blue planet alight in a cosmic sky. She saw the energy beams coming in from Venus with pulsing pathways of support that radiated through the grids and out into the webs that connected Earth. Earth's Torus was lighting up, Gaia was receiving and transmitting, merging and blending, then extending herself as an awareness deep into the galactic fields. In this new pattern, Celestia saw also how the Earth-Sun was connected to the Great Central Sun, which she observed, was like a white hole in the middle of the Galactic Centre.

Everything seemed to be in flux as the membranes of the people on Earth were recalibrated with Earth's own new pattern. This was in turn recalibrated into the Solar System membrane, which then recalibrated itself into the universal and then merged with the membranes of the interdimensional multi-verses.

These in turn flowed on like undulating waves, to recalibrate the position of the universe into a different space and dimension within the very weave of creation.

To Celestia, it was all a dancing flow of color and light that was filled with sound waves of tones and vibrating patterns of movement. These coalesced to radiate energy streams that changed life moment by moment in both grand and subtle ways. All of it was spellbinding and the unfoldment before them was truly grand! Yes, Earth's children, were finally growing up and it was clear that many had joined Gaia on her journey back to realms of light.

Celestia also knew from her interactions with many on Earth that some could not transition for it was not their time to do so. From this perspective, this too was fine, as the fields above her reflected the thoughts she held deep inside. Slowly she began to see another Earth appearing, like a shadow of its new self. This was the old Earth of duality that was now being made even denser again by Gaia's flow to a field of higher light.

Two Earths had formed.

In one vision, Celestia saw the separation of the flows of love and fear and how some would stay behind to learn more of the dual-natured tides. She saw how all of it was perfect, how all was done with each one's free will aligned to fulfill pre-destined agreements.

She looked closer at the image of the two Earths before them, noting how one was much denser than the other was. They looked so similar yet on one the light shone so much brighter and lives were moved by the flows of Grace and care. She noticed then the doorways between these Earths, which appeared like bridges of light. Each bridge was filled with people moving up and on or walking between the worlds as those whose job it was, moved back and forth to guide the ones who were open to ascend. It was time for all to choose the path of love or fear for soon the doors between these worlds would be closing.

Celestia relaxed as the scenes above continued to shift and she sensed how Earth's rising would have an impact on them all.

Tao Lao had recently told them that over time various rules had been given, invitations issued and held, so that Earth's membranes had shifted and the flows had become richer again. He said that this was always the way of the fields when a planet's spirit returned itself and its people back home.

As they watched, Celestia, Tan and Matthias, all realized their end game, while also seeing that it was in truth, just a new beginning. The fact that Gaia's rise had triggered the transformation of the Universal membrane was a bonus, no wonder the auditorium had been buzzing! If all happened as they had seen, it was destined to be a truly wondrous time for all!

~*~

A few rows away from the Earth Delegation, Sarah sat with Marselan. As the presentation about Earth came to a completion with questions asked and answered, Sarah felt a surge of pride igniting deep within her that released a call to remember more of her life as Rani.

Still, whatever her memories revealed, nothing would affect her new creations for never had she felt so alive and so fulfilled. As she sat quietly with the one who'd claimed her heart she sensed again that they were bonded from way beyond the stars, where time could hold no form. Yesterday was gone and her future would be a very loving co-creation regardless of her past.

~ 22 ~

Tan

Leaving the dais, Tan took his seat beside Celestia who was beaming in delight. He smiled at her then closed his eyes, took a few deep breaths to align more with his pure Essence inside and less with a potential ego high.

The presentation had occurred uniquely for them all. As Matthias spoke, the energy fields above him had ignited, revealing so much more. All of their code-work had clicked in, with their educational programs developed, released and applied. Networks had unified to support that which was beneficial to all and so they had helped to turn the tide. What they had just witnessed had confirmed this and much more.

With his eyes, still closed Tan let it all go, the work, the assessments, and the ride, all of it he surrendered to his breath.

Breathe up Essence, slow inhale, relax into it, slow exhale. He soon felt it humming within him, a sweet pulse of love deep inside and into the silence of its rhythm with his breath he began to dive.

Relax, just BE ... was the thought he held in his mind and in this, he stayed. *Breathe, just breathe.*

Within his breath, he was not Tan, brother then lover to Rani his intended bride, taken by a sea with a stronger tide. Nor was he Mary's foundling son, left on the doorstep of her life.

He drank in more of his own pure Essence letting it rise to strengthen and align him again from deep inside. On each exhale he let it all go, the roles of lover, brother, son, orphan and friend, all he had been to Loki, all his training with Hosho and Tao Lao.

In each breath he just let go, replacing the spaces of old memories, filling every cell with just the Essence of his life.

He felt it then, a little way up and over to his right, a row or two ahead, a sweet and loving pulse that connected with his heart. Intrigued he opened his eyes and was drawn like a magnet to a head of long darkish sun-bleached hair, more golden than Rani's was; with a rounder, more dark skinned face. With a profile so like the girl he had loved, this one was a fuller bosomed, more muscular version of his Rani. He stared at the woman for a while until she turned to stare back in his eyes. He felt something shift between them then shook his head dismissing the thought that it could be Rani. She smiled then turned back to talk to the one beside her, the man Matthias had long called friend.

"His new wife is with him, it seems that they have a young child. She reminds me of photos you've shown me of Rani ..." Matthias had said to Tan about Marselan the previous night.

All of this he thought as he noticed the quiet acceptance in his heart, which had not responded as expected at the idea that if this, was his Rani that she could be with someone else. Instead, he only felt a desire for Rani to be happy.

At this exact moment, Celestia released a sweet and happy sigh. "Isn't this just the best day ever? Am I right? Yep, I'm right!"

And so it was to Celestia, that Tan now turned and smiled.

Feeling unsettled by the young man's gaze Sarah sensed that this was the young man who was her baby's father. *Tan, his name is Tan,* an inner voice now told her.

Apollo was Tan's; she saw that now, for his face was reflected in her sons. She took a few deep breaths as the memories rose within her; walking on a moonlit beach, swimming in warm waters, making love with a rhythm that lacked the passion that she shared with Marselan.

Tan was a brother and not a lover desired. And in that moment she made the decision that, only Marselan would help to raise her child. Yes, Apollo would have Tan's inquisitive mind, his sense of compassionate care for others in his world but from Marselan, Apollo would know enough to never tread the path to war. They would raise him a diplomat, like Matthias Inshallah, whom Sarah had admired at first sight. As her memory returned, she knew that Matthias had loved Tan like a son until his healing was done. She sensed then that Tan was finally free from missing her and so she could also now embrace a brand new future that was free from concern of the past.

Strange she thought, that just one look could unlock the memories that had eluded her for so long.

Stranger still that she had no desire to even see again or talk to the one she now knew that she had once loved. It was as if her past had been a dream and that Marselan's presence back on Earth had called her to reawaken. His presence on the island had called her back again, she knew that now, for it was if they truly were two halves of a much stronger magnetic whole.

~ 23 ~

That night Sarah made another dreamtime visit to her mother's world, meeting with Mary in that space between the realms, that some called lucid dreaming. Something had shifted within her for with the return of her memory of Tan, came the memories of her mother. In a dream she would remember, Sarah travelled by the speed of thought from the Arcturian Congress to Australia. She felt like a heat-seeking missile set to connect with her mother, to be Earth bound in an instant.

"Ahh," she sighed descending over the east coast of the great island, gliding in past the Byron Bay lighthouse with its ley line portals of entry. Stepping through the coastal matrix, she found herself with Mary, who was playing with high-pitched tones.

There Sarah waited as the silent watcher, while the voice of her mother joined the keyboard chords to re-energize Earth's fields.

As the sound reverberated through her, Sarah felt as if her whole being was being reformed and as the final adjustments were made, her presence as Rani was revealed.

Mary looked up to exclaim, "I knew it! I knew you'd come back and this time remember!" and within seconds they were locked in each other's embrace.

Her mother had put on weight – she felt good – more solid and round but then so had Rani. With her chest filled with milk for her child and her hips and bottom rounder.

Mary sensed it straight away, "How is my grandson?"

"You know of this?" her daughter asked, perplexed.

"This is not our first visit on the dreamtime plane, just perhaps the first we'll both fully remember!" she lovingly responded. "So how are the men in your life?"

"Apollo and Marselan are both fine."

"You look well my darling daughter, unsettled but well …"

"I've just seen Tan; he's at the Congress I'm attending with Marselan within the Arcturian sector. He looks well, I think he's in love again or beginning to be …"

"I assume it's with Matthias Inshallah's daughter?" Mary stated.

"I think it's her – they make a good couple – she looks besotted with him and he, well, not too sure. Too soon to say I think for Tan."

Mary watched and listened so happy her daughter had come home and that this dream was in fact a very lucid bilocation.

"And you and Jacob? How are you both?"

"It's nice here, peaceful, we like living on the land."

"You don't miss it? All the travelling plus your life in Paris? I know you loved Montmartre."

"Do you miss your old life Rani? With Tan and your plans?"

"I haven't had time to; I'm only just remembering bits and pieces. Nothing yet of my childhood, only that you and Tan were part of it. It feels like I was transported to another world, stepped into another life … Marselan and I … we are not just soul mates or twin souls but a perfect fit... He loves Apollo as his own and me as if I am the most precious being in the whole universe. He is tender, self-assured … much older than Tan. Losing my past like that, having no memories, made it so easy to fall back in love with him, at least that's what it feels like … that I just fell back in love …"

Rani's energy fields were pulsing, sparkling with color as she spoke of the one she now loved. It was obvious to Mary that her daughter had finally found the right one for her heart. It was never like that with Tan who was more friend and companion than someone who could fire up Rani's soul.

"Tell me about the baby … who does he take after?" Mary whispered, her own heart filled with love.

Rani studied her mother's face then smiled, "You."

"Me?"

"Yep you. I know Tan is not your bloodline but I am. It was so obvious when I saw Tan today that Apollo is his child. Still now that I see you, I can say he has your heart-shaped face, the slope of your eyes – though Apollo's are the same color as Tans. He has the cutest little nose, very aquiline like mine I guess. Your skin color, not Tan's or mine, hair a little wavy like his father's but lighter like yours."

"You'll bring him to us soon? And Marselan? Come and stay awhile?"

Rani nodded, tears were filling her eyes. "We'd love that."

As Mary waited for Rani to regain her composure, she began to share more of her life. "You'll adore it here; there is enough land for Jacob to grow everything from sunflowers to pumpkins and herbs. He still won't eat anything he grows so the local wildlife is happy. I dance a lot more these days and do so much now on the inner planes, have long periods of silence, no real travelling anymore. But I love it all. So I guess that answers your question! Do I miss my old life? No, Rani, like you, I've just moved on.

"It's nice to be self-sufficient and be so close to the land. Gaia's spirit is strong here – a good place for children to grow. Apollo will love life here I'm sure, we'll make this his second home ..." she paused then for a few moments of comfortable silence, sensing Rani was ready to speak.

"We've been living on an island, in the Tyrrhenian Sea. Marselan calls it Avalon. He comes from Orion; you know one of his smaller starships came and got us, beamed us up effortlessly and in the blink of an eye transported us to the Congress! Apollo loved it all just as I'm sure he'll love it here!"

They both felt so much lighter as they shared throughout the night, reunited and so loved.

~ 24 ~

"You're a happy one this morning!" Marselan noted as Sarah bounded out of bed filled with the joy of her remembrance.

Marselan was just waking and still looked half-asleep, his hair tousled, the faint shadow of a silver beard now etched upon his face.

"Stay there," Sarah smiled and kissed him. "I'll change Apollo, then bring him back to bed – there's stories to tell!"

"You've remembered more?"

"Let's just say it's time for our son to meet his grandmother and you, your parents-in-law!"

"Well we're not really married yet are we?"

"In all but name my sweet and we can do that there if you like – Mum will be ecstatic! When can we return?"

"To Earth?" he teased, enjoying her excitement.

"Of course to Earth!"

"Well the island I found you on is not my home as you know my love, it is a place of healing … come to think of it, and I can't remember when I had a home …"

"So we can return soon can't we? Surely, you won't go back to war? And if you no longer go to war, you won't need healing or the island, unless we want to be on Avalon for holidays? Take a moment, think about it?"

As she left their room to collect and change her son, Sarah was startled at the thought that Marselan might even think to go back to his old life, for intergalactic warfare was even more deadly than the wars still fought on Earth. One push of a button could annihilate a whole planetary system and fighting for peace made no sense to any of them anymore.

"Well …" Marselan began as she came back to their room. "You're right, things are different now so it's time to talk this through. I'm tired of war and I couldn't imagine my life without you."

"Great that's settled then! Resign from your commission and relocate permanently to Earth!"

Marselan laughed at her determination thinking how could he refuse. With her, he was a lover not a fighter after all. "Okay," he smiled, "I have a meeting with Matthias later, and he's already asked me to be a liaising force for the Embassy of Peace on Earth and our Orion brethren. No doubt, there's a lot Earth can learn of what not to do from what we've done in our system! I guess that it would still mean a lot of travel but I would be more of a peaceful diplomat again."

"Okay, sounds like a plan!" Sarah smiled and kissed him with great passion, then settled back to feed her hungry son as they made more detailed plans.

"I guess that we could find a base on Earth, live close to your parents if you like? Then maybe you could travel sometimes with me?"

"And Apollo?"

"When he's able ... when it's right for us all to do so?"

"When can you arrange it?"

"Today? Tomorrow at the latest! Soon enough for you?"

"Perfect! Wow I'm going home and you're going to meet your nana!" she laughed as she lifted her son in the air.

~ 25 ~

Sarah was silent, deep in her meditations as Marselan later toured the complex with Apollo. The city was grand enough to be almost overwhelming. Light and spacious, crystalline in structure, it operated as a responsive interactive hologram, barely there. Everything undulated around them, always ready to morph and change its view as if existing only to serve and please the viewer.

Those who needed the peace and quiet of the elements of water, earth, fire or air, would find themselves surrounded by the ideal of what they sought. And so it was that Sarah had learnt how to go back to her island's birthing pool via her meditations.

It began the morning they had arrived as she was bathing Apollo in their apartment. Even though they were in a top floor unit with impressive views over the city, as she bathed him that day her mind had wandered back to the women of the glade, that magical place where Apollo had been born. She felt as if all the songs they had sung to her through that long night of labor had been imprinted in her veins and so she had sung these melodies every time she bathed him.

Sometimes in the singing, Sarah found herself transported there again. No longer in labor, instead the fields had shifted to appear as her time was now; same timeline, different view. And so they'd spent that first morning bath time physically at the Arcturian Congress while they played together in spirit in the pools beside the birthing pond where the women gathered time and time again to bring a new soul to their world. Sometimes the women came just to sing and with their heartfelt singing, their voices would merge to reweave Earth's fields.

With that first transportation to the glade, Sarah and Apollo had sat waist deep, splashing the water in play, feeling the warm rays of the sun soak through their skin until it glowed like gold.

There birds sang and swooped around them or settled on the rocks close by to talk of things they knew, for in this place all could hear the words that bird songs held.

They loved these bathing times when the veils would part and Sarah could step back into their world for Apollo would shine even brighter with each visit.

"He is of our tribe," they had once told her, "welcome anytime."

Earlier that day when Marselan had told her of his meeting and Apollo had clung to his arms wanting to be wherever this big man would go, Sarah had smiled and wished them well, happy to spend some time alone for she was missing the quiet of their island home.

Feeling drawn to meditation Sarah sat in the silence and opened to just be. Breathing out, she let it all go, her past, their future, her joy at remembering Mary in the dreamtime.

She thought about the ones she loved, then let the loving of them go to relax deeper with each slow exhale. On each deep gentle intake of breath, she imagined drawing up from her core the pure Essence of her being.

Just be ... she told herself. *Nothing to do, all is well now ... just be,* and so she relaxed into that peaceful place inside. Some magical moments later, she found herself back among the women of her island's birthing pool.

None had seemed surprised when her holographic form had materialized once more among them; most had simply nodded as if her return was the most natural thing in the world. And so they sat in silence under a starlit Earth sky surrounded by those that always come to be the silent witness.

"You have come far," one of the Elders spoke clear and true mind to mind.

Sarah allowed herself to drift mentally and relive what had occurred since they'd left the island; their starship beam-up, their quick arrival into another dimension where the Congress was held, the Congress itself and all that was shared about Earth.

"The Rainbow Serpent has risen. It is time, all is well ... " the Elder women intoned as they tuned to all that Sarah's mind was sharing. When the last image faded from her mind drumbeats slowly began to pierce their silent glade and one by one, the women rose to dance. It felt

celebratory, victorious, as if Sarah was watching the final stages of something long destined to unfold and the glory that this brings.

Refreshed by her meditations, Sarah completed her inner plane journey just as Marselan and Apollo returned, bright-eyed and enchanted by all that they'd both seen.

"You're happy!" she laughed.

"Never thought I'd live long enough to see it. Knew what we were all trying to accomplish, but I wasn't sure I'd ever see it actually occur. Talk is everywhere Sarah!"

"About what is going on with Earth?"

"And more … come, you'll see, everyone seems to be gathering in the foyer!"

~ 26 ~

Marselan was right, their foyer was now buzzing; filled with beings whose light shone brightly through eyes that sparkled like jewels in a sea of color.

Some beings around them radiated a spiraling flow of rainbow light, acting like the energy field fine tuners, which they were, and Sarah sensed that their rhythm had long been programmed to a healthy harmonious existence.

Other beings shone iridescent around her as if they'd shed an outer layer of skin; she was sure none of them had looked like this at the Congress.

To Sarah, all of them undulated as a shifting energy flow even Marselan and Apollo. She stopped, breathed slow and deep, and then noticed the shivering shifting currents in her own body as something began to rise a little within her. It felt as if her Essence was singing, vibrating through her with a stronger feel and beat.

Now, as the trio drifted through the room everyone's membrane shifted with like attracting like as the Goddess of Fate revealed her hand.

Apollo was transfixed, Marselan was proud and strong, and she was fluid and graceful. Sarah could feel it all. She noticed how the energy flow around her held the conscious awareness of every experience that each one in the room had ever lived and as their membranes continued in the merging so did all their stories.

Sarah saw it all so clearly, as if a matrix of colored energy flows was superimposed in her mind and over her eyes. The flows around her were becoming crystal clear, filled with a deeper inner light as everyone's true nature was revealed with a smile, a nod or a glance.

As they continued to weave through the crowd, she whispered up at Marselan, "Just being in this field, it's changing us, you are both morphing before my eyes!"

"You look like an intergalactic princess – you truly do!" he beamed then kissed them both with a tenderness and calm. "Do you remember us now?" he whispered in her ear.

All of it Sarah now saw as if veils were being parted. They had begun it here, in this city of light, eons of Earth time ago. Here they'd been scientists of the higher light, working side by side.

"We left all of this?" Sarah marveled beginning to realize who they truly were.

Marselan nodded then sighed. "Just relax, you'll remember why …"

"But it feels as if we never left, that we are also still alive here, loving our lives here …"

She felt a hand on her shoulder and was gently turned around. "We are … still here," she added as she stared at a slightly older mirror version of herself who was with a slightly older version of Marselan.

Sarah reached out; her hand went through them, their holograms aglow.

"I'm Ra-Aniel … this is Mars," the woman was a field of shimmering light that held a face that looked like Rani. "Your birth name is Rani, you now call yourself Sarah, which name shall we use?"

"Sarah, will be fine for the moment," she said feeling a little overwhelmed and unusually tongue-tied. The duo before them was enchanting. "Why?" was all she could ask. "Why did we leave all of this, especially to come into the denser planes of Orion and Earth?"

Ra-Aniel smiled like the sunshine on a beautiful summer day. "There was a need for the seeding to be done from many dimensions. Everyone who came to Earth volunteered to do so. From our realms, it is easy to send just a part of ourselves down through the dimensions into denser form. So when the opportunity came up, we discussed it, and here you are returned."

"I felt you often with me, I see this now – guiding me, loving me …" Sarah added softly.

"Always," Ra-Aniel smiled. "Though you lost contact with us from time to time. I believe being in Earth's energy field does that with most that go to Earth from the higher realms."

Sarah felt that she'd know the one before her anywhere. In her deepest meditations, this was the membrane into which she'd always melt and merge; this was the inner rhythm whose beat she tried to be anchored in through her journey through the realms. Ra-Aniel was right, many forgot, she'd forgotten, she saw this now as plain as day. She and Ra-Aniel were one and here they stood in another part of a huge Tapestry of Creation in a dimension much more loving and aware.

The more the consciousness of her own vast being expanded itself the more Sarah saw the story of it all. She was just a point of light in a web of light that also held waves of sound. She felt that the flow of her Essence was woven through creations web. She was the light, the darkness and more so she shifted views to look back through her tapestry of life and moved her awareness back to Earth.

"Brave … some said," Marselan noted breaking into her visionary stream.

"Foolish perhaps," Ra-Aniel acknowledged, "or so it may seem to you now."

"No I get it …" Sarah smiled relaxing back into their field. It was as if they were all reabsorbing each other as their memories and insights merged.

"As Sarah, I am just one river or extension of our vast ocean Essence self …"

"See it like sun rays," Mars grinned, then added, "our Essence is a sun that shines out rays of light. The portion of the light ray that is closer to its source can obviously hold more light.

"As the light descends it identifies less and less with its inner nature as it enjoys the outer realms and exchanges energy flows with other light rays along the way – interacting via the blending of membranes and tones.

"Eventually the ray of light begins the return through the dimensions to its Source where it brings back all it has known and been imprinted by."

As Sarah watched the older version of her love speak so eloquently about the matter of their creation, an energy began to rise within her, an essence so pure that was moving her beyond all the boundaries that she had ever known. It rose and sparkled throughout her to infuse her DNA and in this space, Sarah claimed her right to be Rani again.

Rani by name was Ra-Aniel through and through, a force of brilliant light now wrapped in human form.

Unhindered by time or space constrictions, Sarah as Rani grew and grew as this Beingness expanded out within her to reconfigure her system. She drifted then in her mind's eye to sense the vastness of her total Essence Being and in this space of awareness, she relaxed. She was love, the beloved, and more; she was light and its darkness, grace in motion, fluid of form, a sparkling iridescence that bubbled through an infinite cosmic sea.

Entranced, she'd long zoned out of the conversations around her as she opened further to feel all that she was and had been.

"Sarah?"

She heard his voice as a distant echo.

"Sarah? Honey?"

It came again. As Marselan touched her arm, she felt herself contracting to come back into her form again, her body shuddering as her spirit readjusted itself back inside. A few moments later, she slowly opened her eyes to sense Ra-Aniel and Mars beginning to fade before her. "We are here, always here," they whispered as they touched their hearts and then they were gone.

And in these moments, she saw that it didn't matter who she loved; all that mattered was that her heart loved fully and felt free.

And in the flow of love of her own creator Being, Rani's heart merged with Sarah's old pure soul. "Love is love is love," it sang from deep within her. "Love is love is love ..."

As if to add a new perspective, Matthias Inshallah suddenly appeared at their side, looking even more regal than usual. He too had a special glow about him, the auric field of a being of light.

"You too?" Marselan laughed.

"Seems so! Seems crazy I agreed to leave this realm behind but we haven't really left at all had we?" Matthias queried.

Marselan laughed. "I think we are just living simultaneous lives, no wonder we all feel familiar! Isn't that your daughter Matthias? Is that her new young man? Why, they are both positively gleaming!"

"Aren't we all!" Matthias added as he looked over to see Tan.

"Well Commander Inshallah, my friend, it seems that congratulations are in order! You must be thrilled how the Congress has unfolded!"

"Yes, especially with the idea of having you based on Earth with your wonderful family!"

~ 27 ~

Tao Lao

Extensions of Essence was how creation formed as flows of consciousness were extended out from the Source. Those aware used this skill with wisdom creating new worlds and new lives to explore.

Tao Lao was no exception. Meditating in his chamber, he assessed the day's events, please at how the Congress was unfolding. The delegation from Earth had caused a level of excitement he hadn't seen in ages. The experiment on Earth was coming to completion and success would soon be theirs!

The monk stopped his thought train bringing his mind back to focus on his breath, watching its natural rhythm while he took this time to relax. In the last few days, he'd been busier than ever.

His work with Isabella in the Middle East had been consuming, taking him away from the more relaxed rhythm of life that he usually held. He couldn't remember the last time he'd been able to sit and just be empty, to feel the Essence of his soul.

Breathe, just breathe, again he let his thoughts flow up and out as he focused on his breath feeling another energy flow in as music and laughter began to fill him instead.

Life was simpler when he lived in his gypsy life timeline where 8tlan was his Rosalina, so now and then he would allow himself the pleasure of moving into this parallel life. It was this life that called him now.

In this realm an aspect of themselves lived fully, so passionate and alive. In this parallel life they danced and sang, and sometimes fought, and always enjoyed good loving. To Tao Lao and 8tlan, this alternate life was a work in progress that was just for fun, to enjoy another rhythm to their lives.

This is what Ra-Aniel and Mars had done to create lives as Rani and Marselan. It was what many from the higher dimensions did, sending a portion of themselves as a beam of light down into denser realms, to serve an evolving planetary system. To the sender, it added another dimension and flavor, one they could zero into from time to time, to support and enjoy vicariously.

They'd forgot, of course, these denser extensions of their higher selves, nearly all forgot they were one with all life in the matrix of creation. They'd forgot they were free to move their consciousness way beyond their physical form as if it were elastic and that they could travel faster than the speed of light by thought alone to find their higher self creator levels and be as one again.

Most extensions got trapped along the way, in denser cycles of karmic ties, forgetting both universal law and that they were Gods in form, divine beings whose makers lived in higher dimensions of light that were held so deep within them.

Seeing Marselan had triggered it all again, for his Sarah had reminded Tao Lao so much of Rosalina. Wild long hair, the dark olive skin and big bright eyes, with a look that came from a woman totally focused on enjoying the fullness of life and the pleasure that living a life in love contained. This version was so unlike the Rani he had known and so much more like the free spirit of his Rosalina.

Rosalina and Tama, yes it was a fun life to play in, almost like a permanent vacation from the service world they knew. In this life, they were two who played with the fire of passion, creative, emotive and free.

Tao Lao had long discovered that freedom meant so many different things to everyone. To those he supported on Earth, freedom meant being able to live in peace, to raise families without fear of war or famine. To those at the Arcturian Congress, freedom meant the ability to be who they all truly were – divine beings of infinite love and wisdom who could meet to support the rising of new worlds, just as Earth was rising now.

To Rosalina and Tao Lao as the gypsy Tama, freedom meant no more persecution. It meant the right to travel where the wind blew them, in peace; able to enjoy the land and each other. In this life, they were not service bound yet nor were they bound by their senses. In this life, they were free to love each other fully and Tao Lao noticed now that he seemed to tune more to that life whenever he needed a bigger dose of 8tlan when they could not physically meet.

Tao Lao closed his eyes, focused fully back into that gypsy timeline called by a longing in his heart to dance, to sing, be free and to connect with 8tlan as Rosalina. They called it their resting life and he realized then the he'd missed being with 8tlan. The multi-universes were vast in their expression especially when one also traversed the dimensions and both of them were busy.

For a moment, their images flashed before him, Rosalina with her long black tangled mess of curls and sharp green eyes that seemed always alight with mischief, her deep throaty voice with its sensual undercurrents that never failed to stir. 8tlan looking like the super efficient Commander of the Starship Elysium that she was, her razor sharp intelligence and knowledge of energy field science; the way all of this would slip aside to reveal the soft sweet core of the woman she was in his arms.

He lingered for a moment in these feelings then tuned his thought stream back to the Starship, sending out his heartfelt love until they connected again.

"Hey ... " he sighed softly as he made contact with 8tlan.

"Hey yourself ... "

"Been busy?"

"Always ... and you?"

"Missing you ... "

And so they spoke mind to mind across the vast dimensions, showing each other mental images of the time that had unfolded since they'd last been as the lover's they were.

"I think I've seen Rani, or at least a version of her, made me think of you ... " Tao Lao stated as he engaged more of 8tlan's mental attention. She'd been working and wasn't quite done.

"Are you still in class?"

"Yes but I'm nearly done ... " she responded mind to mind.

"Subject?"

"Interdimensional Energy Field Dynamics as it pertains to Living Backwards in Linear Time zones."

"Have you got time for me once you've dismissed the class?"

"Sure ... okay done ... I'm all ears. Where did you think you saw Rani? At the Congress?"

"With Marselan, Inshallah's friend, they have a child, she looks different, reminded me of Rosalina ..."

8tlan could sense his longing for her and smiled. She began to tune herself in to Rosalina and Tama's timeline, could sense him there with her. If they couldn't be together here, they could be together there, if only for a while.

~ 28 ~

8tlan

Now as 8tlan, she danced under a star-filled sky lit bright by a moon that was full. In circles she twirled, spinning around the outside of the fire as others clapped or stamped old feet or rose in song to join her. Heat was growing around them infusing the field with a trance-like flavor.

Yes, life was good in that realm. As Rosalina she drank it in, smiled when she thought she saw Tama watching from where he always did, somewhere in the background.

She closed her eyes and let the music take her on a journey through the stars. She danced with Isis in Egypt and in Atlantis when she'd been pure harmony and tone; she danced at the time of the Christ before the conflict had come. So many lives, so many dances. Rosalina sensed herself expanding further out among the stars, her spinning more fast and furious as she surrendered into trance. She danced then, in the middle of the cosmos, feeling the ecstatic joy of the flow.

Soon many others had joined her, finding their own space and rhythm as the music transported them all and in their mind, they became the cosmic wanderers of old. Each full moon they danced to do just this, to change their earth-bound rhythms and play out among the stars, free from their bodies and lives.

Dressed in the form of Tama, Tao Lao had waited for the dance to stop and for Rosalina to fully come back into her sweat-drenched body. This sometimes took awhile, so now he waited patiently under the tree that they'd loved ever since they were both small children. As he watched and waited for his love, he let his mind go back to when contact had been made with the gypsy elder; a spritely, priestly-type man who had Rasputin's glow. "Good hearted," 8tlan had said.

"What will you bring to this ragtag gypsy band?" the old one had stated as he'd sensed them both zoom in on that first day of meeting.

They adjusted their holographic images to stabilize themselves further into the energy field of the ones beside the fire.

"We seek only to be born into your tribe and have a life of peace and pleasure. Our presence will offer the same to all for as long as we remain among the tribe and hopefully long after as we blend our ways ..."

"You can guarantee the end of our persecution?" someone had asked in disbelief yet full of hope.

"We can ensure you are never where trouble is found unless ... you wish to find it!" Tao Lao added with a chuckle to soothe the crowd. His manner was always diplomatic and relaxing.

At this point 8tlan had spoken, "As I grow I wish to be again with herbs and healing salves, to later midwife your women and bring your children safely into this world."

The gypsy women looked up and nodded their heads, muttering how much this would be needed. By then, their own midwife would have just passed on leaving none who had a calling to the work as the band had long been scattered with the conflicts they'd endured.

"Keep us out of trouble's way? Make life long?" the old one had asked skeptically.

"Maybe," Tao Lao grinned, "if a long life is not in your contract, then at least pleasure will abound! Still you seem to have both my friend. So we will come?"

"Done!" the Elders had agreed as their inner eyes filled with a light of understanding about these ones from the stars.

Their extensions came in together as friends will often do, and so 8tlan was called Rosalina and Tao Lao became Tama.

Born to an elderly couple, who had never been with child, a ray of 8tlan's light had blended with the budding babies DNA as a single cell became two then doubled again to eventually form a sweet girl-child. Pure of heart she was programmed for the pleasure of a healthy, light-filled life that was there to benefit others, a life to be filled with love.

8tlan's energy had been present and deep within Rosalina all the time, just like an angel spirit guide, and yet it was more than this for even as a baby Rosalina retained full memory of all that they had done.

Tao Lao's mother died in childbirth, and cradled by strong loving arms, he had come to bond with his father, to give him the gift of inner sight. As the infant Tama, he would part the veils so that his mother could enter the dreams of his father at night where their life continued on. His father always held a smile on his face as if he was privy to something loved and bright. Never did he grieve for his young wife who he still loved well in his dreaming each night. He spoke of her as if she were alive to keep her so for the child who understood the dreaming and the realms that dreamtime claimed. From the dreaming came all the changes in the worlds. And so just like his father, Tama also enjoyed his mother in their dreamtime world. To this gypsy band, all of this was normal.

They did as they said, these cosmic wanderers from the stars, entering the life of these people who roamed from land to land, never claiming any as their own. They belonged nowhere and to no one but their own.

8tlan and Tao Lao didn't plan the details of if they would reunite to fall in love or just be friends this time yet Tama had always found Rosalina a wonder to behold, especially when she danced. She dispensed the herbs that kept them healthy and brought the wailing new ones to their world, as other star-born joined them.

And with their coming, the band found a rhythm of harmony that was happy and peace-filled for all. It was an abundant life, where prosperity meant trusting in the universal flows of like attracting like and goodness bringing more. Laws were adhered to and practices maintained. Creations were discussed and formed with the rule that all they created would always enhance the whole. It worked and the gypsy band was soon living lives that were filled with pleasure.

"We are lucky ..."

"Blessed ..."

"Taken care of ..." were words they often shared.

For each of them, their consciousness remained elastic, able to shift between the portals of their parallel lives especially when Rosalina danced or blended with Tama in the Tantric way. There, they loved fully, enjoying all the layers, the dance of the life of a couple whose bonds were strong and true. And in the times of their mergings they witnessed it all; their weaves and blends in their tapestries of creation plus how their past and futures were intertwined, simultaneous and connected by the web of life.

~ 29 ~

8tlan & Tao Lao

8tlan came out of her bilocation meditation, happy to return. She loved both lives but this one most of all; holding the Elysium steady in position so close to Earth, still undetected yet effective in repose.

Everything was humming just as Tao Lao had said. In fact, it had been the Starship Elysium that had beamed in all additional imaging to the Congress as Commander Inshallah had shared his view of Earth.

The Cosmic Wanderers were destined to soon be back home with their intergalactic family for millions on Earth knew now that they were just projections of light from the higher dimensional flows.

Millions of Light Beings had taken human form, to be born as babies among the tribes of Earth. They came in as star-children with different strands of DNA and brains hardwired to know the pathways of return.

Other Light Beings would walk among the crowds as children with light-filled eyes, bored easily with the schools they'd come to transform. Still others downloaded from their original planetary systems, new energy devices that would revolutionize Earth's world and eliminate global warming.

Everything was mixing and reforming in the fields as Gaia's Earth as her people were repatterned back into 8tlan's world. The Intergalactic Federation had long been hearing Earth's call, responding accordingly to guidelines of non-interference. Unless changes were asked for, nothing could happen with any emerging world. Most found their way regardless and asking sped the process up so the rising and the merging could occur.

Enough had asked.

Enough had responded.

All was well in their world.

The only thing concerning 8tlan now was whether she should reveal to Matthias, the possible future of his Angel's life. How fixed was this future anyway? And was there anything Matthias could do to prevent it? Was his Angel dying or just sick? They all knew that death was really just an illusion for the Essence nature of each continued on. In body, out of body, it didn't matter in the long run, what mattered was that each fulfilled what they had come to do and enjoyed the journey and the way.

* * *

In another space and time, Tao Lao sat with Marselan and Matthias. The older men spoke freely as Marselan softly spoke of future plans, a place on Earth as an emissary, there to lend a hand.

Sarah sat beside them on the floor near a virtual fire with Apollo asleep in her arms. The child was Tan's, he saw that now and so he ventured into her mind as Sarah closed her eyes.

"Rani?" Tao Lao whispered gently.

"Mmmm ..."

"Don't go too deep in your meditation ... Sarah? Rani?"

"Both," Sarah sighed contentedly in her mind. *"We are both and more."*

He saw it then, how Marselan was Rani's true mate, not Tan. It was clever that, having Rani forget her past so that she could come back freely to this man; free of the past and old memories that constrain.

She was peaceful now, so Tao Lao let his mind drift back through the times the three of them had shared. So much had occurred for them all; meetings, partings, moving on with their new creations, all of them extensions of the Source, all of them with different levels of awareness or concern. Rest lives, play lives, lives of service or learning, all of it broadened and deepened who they were, adding subtle layers to the whole.

He had been trained to see all as one and every ray of light as an extension of pure Source. Ra-Aniel was Rani in yet another form, just as he was with Tama and yet he was them all. Each one of them was the same for without their pure Source Essence none could ever be born.

"So," Tao Lao stated as the meeting wrapped up for the night, "much has been accomplished. Marselan and Rani will return to be based on Earth where both can help with Embassy matters ..."

"Both of us?"

"Yes, my dear Rani," Tao Lao smiled, "for you too have a lot to offer! In time the Embassy will call to you too, once you have some free time from your babies, for as you know there is still a daughter yet to come."

And so he left her then to wonder how life would be living once more so close to Tan.

Sequestered in their quarters, Marselan was radiant as he enfolded her in his arms, "A daughter?" he whispered. "Now that would be a blessing! To have another just like you ..."

"Perhaps in a year or two?" Sarah responded to his kiss.

"The sooner the better for me," Marselan announced as they readied themselves for bed. "How precious can life be ... my sweet, just how precious can our life be? I'd always thought that my exposure to chemical warfare as a young man had taken the prospect of children away!" he sighed.

~ 30 ~

Tan

Tan was pacing in his quarters, his heart pounding in his chest. It was true as he'd thought, Mary had just confirmed it! Rani was alive and also at the Congress. Why hadn't his heart responded when he thought he'd seen her? Had he really let her go? To Tan it seemed as if a door had closed within him, refusing to reopen ... it was not how he dreamed it would be if ever he found her again. Was this Celestia's doing? Had she finally replaced his Rani in his heart of hearts?

No, he decided, it was more than this. Seeing this new version of Rani, a baby in her arms, the older statesman at her side, so obviously in love ... he'd never seen her glow like this, so confident and sure as if she belonged again. He knew then that she'd never been like that with him.

Was this love? To let her go, just happy that she was happy and so free?

Tao Lao had told him of Marselan's arrangement with Matthias – they would soon be neighbors again. He wondered how that would be, to see them at the Embassy on Earth, this happy loved-up family?

Tan searched again, filling his mind with her as he waited for a heart response, surprised again that there was none. He was glad she'd been returned, but even more, he was amazed that there was no longing for her in his soul.

Memories flooded through him of the life they'd known. Their time as children in the Enchanted Kingdom, Seth and the damage he'd caused to them both and all the learning they had gained. He remembered their training with Hosho and time in 8tlan's world aboard the Starship Elysium where they learnt the value of life as a Cosmic Wanderer.

He thought of the walk-in Jacob who had taken over Seth's life, who brought the light of love to Mary's eyes. Images of happy couples flooded through his mind, Tao Lao and the way he looked at 8tlan, the way his Rani as Sarah looked into Marselan's eyes.

He was at peace with it all.

Slowly Celestia's face began to fill his mind and he saw her big bright eyes, filled with love for him. His heart leapt as he knew that at last he'd found it, the permission to move on. He was worthy of the greatest love, Tan saw that now. It was time for his heart to open fully, for his soul to share all he had to give.

Tan was smiling broadly, as he heard the gentle knocking and went to open the door.

"Well don't you look a picture!" he decreed.

There she stood looking like a cosmic princess in a multi-colored gown of flowing silk.

"Don't look too bad yourself!" she smiled as he scooped her up into his arms to melt her into a kiss that was deep and filled with heartfelt longing.

"Wow … not complaining … but are you okay?" Celestia sighed as they finally drew apart.

"Never been better!" he laughed. "Rani's back and I'm free!"

Deep down inside, Celestia sighed in relief for he was kissing her with passion. Nothing else mattered now, except to finally feel his arms so willingly wrapped around her.

"Ready?" he asked her quietly.

"For?"

"The dance tonight at the Congress ballroom and maybe even this dance through life … with me?"

"Definitely in the mood for dancing anytime!" she giggled.

"Good then, I'll introduce you!"

"To?"

"Rani, she's the one they call Sarah."

"Apollo's mother? God that child's so sweet!"

"Yep! Who'd have thought she'd show up again as someone else's wife!"

"You seem good with it …?"

"I am – it's right – she's back exactly where she should be … and so am I!"

Celestia smiled up at him then, her eyes so full of love. Despite their cosmic callings and all they were born to achieve, to her the greatest achievement was to always feel the rhythm of pure love within her heart.

Tao Lao watched it all, this cosmic play unfolding. Yes worlds were born to rise and fall until the final rising. Would the Earth he knew finally make it and take her rightful place among their realms? He sensed so for the Tapestry of Creation was sparkling to match the rising joy within their lives. *Yes,* he sighed, *after so much trial and error the Earth was coming home! And perhaps it was also time for Tan to finally realize just where he had come from.*

While Matthias's Angel had always felt incomplete and searched doggedly to find her mother, Tan had never asked any of them about his origins. Yet Tao Lao knew that it was a subtle longing locked deep within Tan's heart.

~ 31 ~

Tan

"Amazing!"
"Unheard of."
"Mesmerizing ..."
Those were the words being bandied around about Earth the next day as Tan tuned into the Congress to listen to the collective throng.

Some spoke of the intergalactic wars that still raged in their sectors, just like war had raged so often on Earth but Earth, they agreed, was rising, an experiment soon complete.

Technologically advanced but unaware of the more subtle dimensions within, there were many species still caught in the dual-natured realms; trapped in a web of their own construction, as they learnt how to live life beyond limitations and old fears.

As Tan listened, others shared of good times entered into, of peace-filled places long enjoyed but most spoke still of all they had heard about Earth.

"Mass genocide."
"Total disregard of the precious nature of life."
"Self absorbed, asleep."
"Trying hard, huge obstacles."
"So dense, so unexpectedly difficult."
"All to be admired."
"Great to see the rising"
"Can't wait for the complete merging to occur ..."
Of all of this they spoke and also so much more.

To Tan and Celestia, the Congress had an air of excited expectation, the anticipation of an event still yet to be born.

"Ahh, there you are!" Matthias Inshallah regaled as he patted the young man on the back and then hugged his radiant daughter. "Splendid event don't you think? Truly, truly splendid! Shame it's the final day."

As the room hushed and lights were dimmed to welcome the final speaker, Tan closed his eyes to focus, then felt everything around him shift as his thoughts turned to his past and his reality field became fluid. Yes, Mary had found him in a basket at her door but where had he come from? Why had someone given him away? Yes, he'd loved her, yes, he'd loved it when Rani had been born and yes, his life had been so full of love and more, yet now and then, he'd wondered who his real parents were.

"The past is gone," an inner voice told him. *"Just let it all go until only the truth remains ..."* and so he slowed his breathing rhythm to open to the subtle realms within until everything dissolved into pure white light.

Slowly an even brighter column of light began beaming out before him on the inner plane, pulsing with aliveness, loving concern and care. Then, two bright eyes, black as the deepest night sky appeared, each filled with a myriad of brilliant stars which seemed to come in then fade out of existence as Tan the watcher stared.

Then those same eyes blinked and the stars went out as the black changed to sky blue shot through with sunshine on an ocean sea. Shimmering sky then water then sky again as eyes blinked once more to become a cosmos filled with stars.

It was just as he'd seen in his dreams, these same eyes, watching him, loving him, filling his being with knowing while dissolving all the questions that he'd had.

But now as Tan watched it all unfold, slowly this vast Beingness came clearer into view.

"Father?" he whispered hoping it was so.

"My son ..."

In this exchange, Tan felt himself again grow full, as if all of the emptiness that he had ever known was being filled inside him by a rhythm of love and a pulse so sweet that held a bliss-filled knowing.

He was home. And in this realization, Tan felt the rhythm of his heart begin to shift and longing dispersed to melt within him.

He was free. And in this space of freedom Tan could see exactly who he was, where he'd been and why he'd come to Earth and found his way to Mary.

Tan was star-borne, first born on Earth, his father a Being of Light from the Great Central Sun. Along with Rani, Mary and the others, he was just an extension of light, sent to serve, to return Earth to her home.

Tan found himself then walking through a field of light, escorted by his Father's spirit. Energies swirled around him and he began to ascend crystal stairs feeling like a fluid stream of love with eyes alight and wise. Up and up he moved sensing this Being of Light at his side until at the top of the crystal stairs the scene opened up into yet another field of light.

Beings began to gather around him that appeared just like his Father, streams of loving light with eyes of cosmic darkness that held the light of stars.

Tan took his place in the Sacred Circle of Beings that had formed, sensing his Father still beside him. There was no need for words as a feeling of great belonging suddenly engulfed him. He was all of this and more. He was just one of this Sacred Council, a being of light and love, his Father's son on Earth and also in this heaven. He noticed then that a hologram of Earth sat suspended in their centre, as each being irradiated the planet with the nourishment of pure Source love. He knew then that this had been their work for eons of time, to lovingly tend to the Garden of Eden that some had once called Earth.

~ 32 ~

Eden's Garden

Mesmerized, Tan focused further on what the Light Beings were doing, letting all the love he felt for Earth flow into the hologram in the circle. As he opened to join the flow, he began to notice that the Earth hologram also held a hologram of another Earth. From this angle, it looked like an onion whose outer layer represented their perfect world, for the top layer was a bright sparkling paradise realm, which held a rhythm of enlightened fulfillment.

Then this layer peeled away.

The next hologram of Earth shone just a little less brightly as the next Earth hologram within this one shone less brightly again and Tan noticed then how there were so many layers, so many holograms and as each layer was stripped away Tan sensed that each was a field of possibility, a slightly different dimension of expression.

As Tan focused in, his consciousness began to flow through each layer until he came to the Earth of 2012; for every year, every level, every evolutionary stage and every positive advancement had been recorded holographically within these multitudes of Earths.

From this new perspective he could see complete evolutionary cycles and how Earth had been lovingly nurtured to be the Garden of Eden that she was, with single celled organisms growing more complex by the second.

In this holographic energy mix, Tan saw clearly how loving Beings of Light were always beaming in to play with Earth's genetic structure as if they were fuelled by a desire to finally create the perfect species, for these Beings were creator Gods who were born to play this way. He realized now as he sat amongst them that every life created held their own creator God inside.

The movie of Earth's unfoldment continued before them, as the Beings in this Sacred Circle revealed it all again as if Earth was a multi-layered jewel with the brightest layer the one that was first revealed. It seemed to Tan that all these Beings saw was the planet's final potential, and yet there were still so many layers until this stage could come to all who dwelled there now.

"Love will stimulate, fear will stagnate," his Father said into his mind.

Each hologram was rapidly changing as Tan saw how earth-life had begun; then its trials and tribulations as free-will was released as part of this new age of man, a species designed to grow, learn, move forwards or backwards but always move on with their evolution.

Each hologram was slightly different. It was like a fast forward time exposure camera recording life with all its weaves and flows. Lights shone, became dimmer, then shone again and moved on, morphing into something more vibrant again, as their collective thoughts and emotions fuelled these pools of light and mankind's creation rose or fell via shifting currents that added to the tapestry of life.

Now Tan could also see the layers of Earth's potential, how her people had begun to enter through doorways that brought them into realms of peaceful play, where everything was manifest with joy. It was through these open doorways that connected into each holographic expression of Earth, that these Holy Beings now poured their love to feed those that were hungry.

It was perfect, he could see this now. The doorways were open, everything was rising as Gaia and her people received the energy influx that they needed. To Tan it looked as if a purer energy was ascending now through many, spontaneously bursting up from their own inner core. As the holograms evolved, he saw how sadness turned to joy, as smiles lit eyes to reveal the changing consciousness of man.

As he continued to scan the holograms before him, Tan saw how each hologram influenced the other as the people on Earth chose to walk the paths of light and go beyond all fear.

Focused back on the hologram of the Earth where he still normally lived, Tan sensed the very skies around the planet change. Suddenly new portals of light appeared and a myriad of spacecraft were revealed. He sensed then how so many craft had long been anchored in Earth's skies, an octave or so higher than what most could see, invisible yet there; watching and patiently waiting for Earth's people to expand their views.

Tan's mind scanned further now, to sweep his inner vision through all the craft; so many unusual beings all with good hearts, kind eyes, yet held in bodies that many of Earth would react so strongly to in fear, all because they looked different.

"You see?" his Father said sighing in resignation.

"I see."

"Preparation is so important; the fear must be dispersed for true contact to be made. The fields of energy are shifting quickly; Earth is rising as you can see. Soon your skies will be filled with so much more as your people begin to really see the worlds within worlds, the portals within the portals, the dimensions blending and merging. The whole game is evolving quickly and your people must be well prepared.

"But see Tan. Look here and here ..." his Father pointed to pockets of energy that were in the hologram of Earth that represented the time around 2012. *"Fear, pure fear, stimulated by your media's misinterpretation of extraterrestrial life, misinformation from your governments ..."*

Tan thought of all the Hollywood movies that continued to portray the threat of alien invasion as hostile beings who sought to take over the Earth. How more movies were being produced almost like clockwork to condition Earth's people and keep them locked in ignorance and fear. His mind moved to the move *Avatar* and how it had touched hearts, finally portraying the advanced nature of those on a peace-filled world. Yes, there were beings who looked like this and more, every species portrayed in *Star Wars, Star Trek,* all existed somewhere in some realm. They were strangely different yet they were also divine beings in form who were more aware of this than so many were on Earth.

He saw it then, how the opposite was true. Earth, with its warlike people, was far more dangerous to the Universe than any U.F.O's as the collective pulse of the planet was influencing universal flows.

Of course, not all E.T.'s were benevolent; some were just like some people on Earth who were trapped in the cycles of their own limited views. Technologically advanced to create their craft and go exploring, many E.T.'s visited Earth looking for resources from genetic material and more and some of these were still dealing with Earth's governments.

All of this flashed like a movie in Tan's mind as he saw those hungry for power struggle to maintain it in a myriad of ways.

"Fear!" his Father stated, *"Fear can cripple an evolving species! Right now Earth's people need to be better informed so that they can collectively move into a brighter future. When the veils fade between the dimensions, many will succumb to the game of fear unable to sense the beauty that surrounds them. All is there my son, all is there!*

"See my son, how so many already exist in Earth's Eden? Peace is there, paradise, your Kingdom of Heaven is already there. It is just a matter of alignment for the time has come for all to find their way as your Earth is homeward bound."

As his Father spoke these final words, he placed his radiant fingers on Tan's heart to affirm the doorway to heaven within him. And at this light-filled touch, the Earth of Tan's time began to clone herself again, as each hologram reappeared like the layers reforming around the core of an onion. The scene was like the blossoming of a flower, going through its various stages to reveal is complete beauty. Yet the changes on Earth were subtle. With each new holographic layer the Earth became greener more peaceful again as Tan watched the pockets of fear change to pulses of love and understanding. He sensed how Earth's people were evolving, aware of the Source within, that true power comes with remembering how systems crumbled and were reborn as the veils of separation parted.

Layers and layers reformed around the planet, each one a higher octave, and each one contained more light until finally the Earth shone bright before them in her holographic form – unified and whole.

"Remember," his Father reaffirmed, *"the key to Earth being bathed in this greater flow of light begins with the willingness to step into this type of future. This is the final choice of all on Earth, to choose the path of love and rise now or stay behind in the realms of duality and fear. Love or fear, the choice is now quiet simple! Yes many have chosen yet this is destined to be a collective rising!"*

Tan got it. He got it all, and in the blink of an eye, he was freer than he'd ever been. For a few moments, he felt like he was floating like a stream of golden stardust, his molecules rearranged into a flow of cosmic plasma. In this state, he was the fire of creation, alive with intelligent thought, free to create, to express; in this state, he sought out worlds and merging with them, felt them as part of his core. In this new fluid state, a thought would come as a directional flow that then condensed to become matter.

Elements, plant, animal, human, he'd been and explored it all. Now he was Tan again, contained once more in human form, his body of light covered by flesh and more.

He sensed his Father near him, knowing now he was always there. They were all connected by a web of light in which each one formed an energy pattern. It was time for the pattern of Earth to come back to its Eden for homeward bound meant coming back to the original pattern of perfection. Earth's Eden was always there, he knew, just a breath away, an alignment with his Essence.

Tan slowly opened his eyes, feeling reborn and refreshed, all his questions answered. His whole journey on the inner planes had lasted only minutes. Sensing Celestia standing quietly by his side he noticed that she looked more radiant than ever before. Their eyes met then, so clear and bright. Hers with the light of love and knowing, and his with a depth of peace that comes with the light of understanding.

"Remember," his Father's voice rang clear, *"your people must be freed from their ignorance and fear for all to know Earth's Eden! It is already there, it is always there!"*

~ 33 ~

Epilogue

Matthias ...
The Congress had been magical, answering everyone's needs, revealing realities previously unimagined.

Matthias let his mind keep drifting back as the Congress seemed worlds away from him now. He'd heard the news as soon as they'd come back. His Angel had been found and once more, his life had been consumed by the weaves of her creations.

He couldn't remember anything much now of all that had come to pass in the Arcturian system, just that everything had gone so well. He remembered a fleeting stop on the Elysium, where 8tlan had lured him back to spend a night or two. He also recalled Celestia's secret smiles at Tan and the way his eyes followed her around the place, how they disappeared again with Loki and their old gang; yet all of it was blurring now as Angel's face consumed him.

Not long now, he thought as he tucked the sheets around her, then sat and held her hand.

His heart felt empty as he sensed her life force leaving, her body shrinking in response.

"I'm ready," she'd said hoarsely whispering late one day and yet she lingered on. Matthias sensed she was waiting for Celestia to come.

"Will you visit?" Matthias asked her later.

Celestia shifted uncomfortably in her seat. "You know I'm no good with people dying," she'd said and yet he knew it was more.

"I'm sorry," she'd admitted. "I can't stand the waiting, it seems like yesterday we were going through this with Mum ... and now this ..."

She had wanted to say that Angel had lived hard and fast, uncaring of so many in her world, or caring too much for others. Up, down, high, low, dramatic in her creation, Celestia never could keep up, never wanted to, and had withdrawn from Angel's scene before her own mother's passing. Celestia was Shaman trained, she liked to use the sacred power plants from time to time but never the chemical combinations that had trapped their Angel.

Angel's scene was never healthy for any one, she'd often thought but always refrained from expressing.

"Just come and say goodbye to her," he'd asked, "I think it will bring you closure."

Matthias was detached yet sad. *Was Angel's life a wasted life?* He mused reflecting on all the opportunities that had come her way. And now his Angel was going with her days unfolding fast, offering precious times to bond again from heart to heart. The past was gone, each moment left, surreal. *It was what it was,* he'd decided and strangely this thought gave him comfort, as did the knowledge that her future in spirit form was bright, light-filled, a place for her to rest and renew.

"How are you?" Matthias whispered as he bent low to kiss Angel's cheek.

Her eyes fluttered open, rolling back in her head.

"Not good," she'd sigh at times, or "I'm okay," she'd whisper then slink into another realm again where medication dimmed the flows of pain. Here, Angel was deep in peace, ready and resigned, almost happy as she opened for release. Once more his Angel would do exactly as she pleased for she'd come to Earth so long ago, to play, to be, to tease. They were kindred in spirit Matthias and this girl, the one he'd long adopted into his heart.

He'd tried to be there with his wife, to coach the girl along but their journey had been even harder once the drugs had come. Losing a loved one did that to some he knew, made them search for peace in substances long known for the euphoria they would bring.

How long since she'd had her first taste? he wondered as he looked into Angel's hollowed face as her eyes rolled backwards in her head, twitching now and then to let him know she still had life.

Heroin, crystal meth, uppers, and downers, so many drugs to play with as his Angel went from teenage girl to the old sick woman who lay in the bed. *She looks twice her age,* he reflected at the skeletal figure before him, grey hair and yellow sunken skin stretched tight over the once revered bone structure of her face. She'd been loved, he knew that, she'd taken and given what she could as she fought the demons of her addictions in her quest for peace in life.

Matthias recalled his last meeting with her mother, "I killed him," she'd sobbed, "we had argued at the restaurant … he was flirting with the waitress as usual … I stormed off took a taxi to a friend's … he'd been drinking … we were both so angry … I shouldn't have left him like that … the crash … oh my God he was burnt alive! I'm not fit to care for her Matthias … Angel is much better off without me … you'll give her a good home …" He'd tried, yes, he'd tried so hard but all Angel had longed for was the one she couldn't find.

All of this 8tlan watched now as she helped to prepare the energy fields for Angel's passing. She also opened the field for a miracle to come, so that Angel could heal the wounds of her heart. Her body was frail and shutting down, 8tlan knew she would not choose to stay for this was the future that she'd seen and Angel had done enough with her days.

As she sat in meditation in her chambers on the Starship, 8tlan tuned in to Matthias to sense deeper in his heart. He was at peace, accepting all that was. A logical man who believed enough in his loved ones to let them choose, and then live by each choice, without his judgment of how things should be done.

"They are adults, and from each choice, all learn," he'd once shared. 8tlan admired his emotional detachment; sensed it also in herself yet now and then, she'd feel the waves of emotion that were bubbling in the field. Yes, his Angel was dying, and her choice had long been made.

It was a time of transition through transcendence and the process was well established for them all.

As the Earth moved her spirit self into a realm of brighter light, many upon her would choose to leave. Many had left already. Others were being transcended, allowing their bodies to shift and change, to let go of all that no longer served the new heart commitments made.

The times, 8tlan noted, were once more in flux, especially where Matthias was. 2012, a year of intense transition. Bombarded by cosmic flows as the realms continued to merge, some people's systems couldn't take the influx of new energies while for others their work on Earth was done.

8tlan scanned the fields, so many now were leaving and more would choose to leave each day. Education for women had changed the odds and birth rates had stabilized with new souls coming in to be part of the 'grand alignment' as it would be called later in her time.

From where she sat aboard the Elysium, 8tlan could scan the lines of time as Earth's past, present and future lay clear before her. With this bird's eye view, she saw the trails and weaves that Earth's people created, her third eye open to life's web.

Matthias would grieve in his own silent way, for this daughter who'd searched for what her heart had longed for. Like many, she'd forgotten that she carried the greatest love within her all along.

How many did that on Earth? 8tlan had wondered, *How many become so entranced in the game of external pleasures that they forget the treasures each carry within?*

She scanned deeper through the fields and saw the endless plays. How drugs like opium then heroin would captivate and weaken all resolve, or how fast food diets appealed yet weakened the species even more. Toxic ways of relating, conflicts without resolution, the battles of minds with hearts that called for different ways. Abuse and lack or fear took it all to another level as so many struggled to stay afloat in the rivers of a life that led to suffering as the body temple crumbled with dis-ease.

Angel had played hard and fast burning through her youth as if she'd had endless days. And now in stillness she lay.

The past was quickly forgotten by all who came to visit, their wounds or disappointments left deep within a heart that was now too tender to recall anything but the preciousness of time. She was here now and so were all who'd come to show her of their care.

Beyond the walls where Angel lay life went on as normal 8tlan noted, as she scanned the fields of this time on Earth.

Across the globe, the Euro vision was being readjusted to align policy and system to better serve the whole. In other times and planes people suffered then grew through fortunes lost or gained as others struggled to let go and then move on or questioned what was going on.

Prophecies had been revealed and dissected, ignored or adhered to and changes made. New souls came in and old souls left, tired or just ready for a new game. In a multitude of galaxies, life unraveled and moved on, responding to creation's will and powerful mental games.

To 8tlan, it was endless, as it now was to them all, as stars were born to burn brightly then go supernova and die out. Consciousness moved in waves throughout it all, stopping in life's flows from time to time to rest or play.

Yes, a new world was calling to them all.

As 8tlan sat in deep reflection in her meditations, Matthias reached over and kissed his Angel on the brow as Celestia stood beside him.

"Goodbye sweet soul," he whispered, "we will meet soon enough on the other side." And with the touch of his lips on her third eye, Angel let her spirit soar and fly away.

Matthias sat down on the bed beside the empty shell of the girl he'd always loved. She'd challenged him and made him grow yet he'd seen too much to mourn her for too long.

Just one small drop of her own vast Essence had been in her now lifeless form, but she was much more than this again. In other realms beyond time, she was also a great Being of Light who had chosen to send a small ray of its Essence into form on Earth. They all did this and yet the illusory world of Earth soon claimed them making them forget.

But thanks to his experiences at the Congress, Matthias was awake, and even more aware that life was just a game. Angel's games had claimed her life yet she touched their hearts in so many different ways. She'd been the light of innocence before the darkness had come and now she'd been set free to be the light of wisdom once again.

As he sat in silence, he tenderly held both his daughters hands. He glimpsed it then, a future time where his grandson would come, another rebel with a cause and a penchant for darkness and war.

Marselan's Apollo would be the Prince of Peace while Celestia's boy would be his Angel reborn as the cycles of life flowed on.

~ End of Book 4 ~

Stay tuned for
Book 5 of
the Enchanted Kingdom Series
intertwining the lives of Rani's, Celestia's
and Aphrodite's children!

ELYSIUM
Shamballa's Sacred Symphony

When the Queen of the Matrix returns the King to her heart,
peace will come to all on Earth, regardless of their part.
And when compassion sets the pace, all will find new rhythms,
a peace within, and a peace without, to last beyond millenniums.

The third book in the Enchanted Kingdom series, ELYSIUM continues
the story of Rani and Tan as they discover the pathways to Shamballa
and develop the Heartland Game. Tracked by both the Dark Ones as
well as other Alchemists that are also focused on the merging of the
worlds, in this book we cover the movement of the rapture, Shamballa's
Shadowlands, parallel worlds plus Earth's rise into more civilized
realms. Guided by the futuristic Commander of the Starship Elysium we
also track the story of the immortal monk Tao Lao who moves back in
time to work with Isabella and influence a young bomber who is hell
bent on revenge.

As with the first two books, *Queen of the Matrix* and *The King of
Hearts*, in Elysium we again find stories of love and hardship and
change that are interspersed with esoteric insights to support the rising
of Earth into higher realms.

Shamballa's sacred symphony is crossing time and space,
forming new realities that are led by waves of grace.
Now Elysium is rising as freedom's path is laid,
by those who know how true love's beat is made.

A cross between Harry Potter, Star Wars & the Matrix movies, this
new series also weaves in some of the aboriginal dreamtime legends
while offering powerful metaphysical tools and futuristic insights that
will entertain all ages.

Glossary

OH-OM

The One Heart One Mind Creative force, called God by Christians, Allah by Moslems, the Source of infinite intelligence and love by others. Has many titles throughout the worlds, seen also as a vast matrix type web or Cosmic Computer that shares its software programs with its creation.

Hosho

Inter-dimensional being of great light and Master of Alchemy, one of the Elders, creator of the Cosmic Institute of Alchemy, mentor of Tan and the field fiddlers and the Kosmic Knights. In the Enchanted Kingdom (E.K.) series, Hosho's main teaching facility is located aboard the Elysium, at the Cadet's Space Station as one branch of the Intergalactic Federation of Worlds.

Angel

Goddaughter of Mathias Inshallah.

Apollo

Son of Rani. Named after the god of Peace.

Aphrodite

Represents the bloom of youth and beauty; childhood friend of Loki, Tan and Rani. Mother of Isis, wife of Loki.

Celestia

Daughter of Mathias Inshallah. Trained onboard the Elysium. Interdimensional Energy Field scientists and peace emissary.

Isabella

Appears in book 3, Ambassador of Peace working with Tao Lao.

Jacob

Walk-in of Seth from book 2. Partner to Mary. Father of Rani.

8tlan

Commander of the Elysium Starship, mentor to Tan and Rani, lover of Tao Lao, future-self connection of Mary, Ambassador for the Intergalactic Federation of Worlds.

Marselan

Intergalactic warrior from the Orion star system. Essence extension of Mars.

Mary
Mother of Rani, surrogate mother of Tan, wife of Jacob. In book 1 & 2, Mary was the over-lighting guide to Agra, represents the one who descends from light into matter.

Matthias Inshallah
Ambassador of Peace on earth. Union of Nations Earth contact for 8tlan and Tao Lao, appears first in book 3.

Loki
Represents the Norse God of Mischief. Tan and Rani's childhood friend, lover of Aphrodite, brother to Leila. Father of Isis.

Queen of the Matrix
The Supreme heart of love and intuition that acts like glue in the web of life. The field of love, that is the Queen, provides the emotional resonance of the fabric of life.

Tao Lao
The one holding the energy of St. Francis and Lao Tzu. Tan and Rani's first mentor and guide, companion to the great grey wolf.

Rani
Mary and Jacob's daughter, protégé of Isis and Tan's adventurous playmate. Visionary and seer, co-creator of the Heartland Game. Essence extension of Ra-Aniel. In book 4, also known as Sarah.

Tan
Mary's foundling son, a master field fiddler in training, Hosho's protégé and Rani's non-blood brother. Childhood friend to Loki and Aphrodite. In book 3, Tan is the co-creator - with Rani and 8tlan - of the Heartland Game. In Cosmic Wanderers, he is the liaising Ambassador between the Embassy of Peace on Earth and the Starship Elysium.

The Elders
Beings of Great Light and love that are focused, like Hosho, on watching and supporting the merging of the worlds.

Volcan Lords
Representation of the darker worlds and the lower consciousness or shadow side of the undeveloped human. Also known as the Dark Ones who worship the lower Gods of sex, money fame and power.

Yesif
Suicide bomber martyr, pawn of the Volcan Lords, appears in book 3.

Terms Used and Context Meant:

Ascension:

The unification of all aspects of our being back into the experience of infinite love and Oneness. Like enlightenment, this is a journey, not a destination, as we can always expand our awareness through the fields to grow and receive more.

Akashic Records:

http://www.edgarcayce.org/about_ec/cayce_on/akashic/

The Akashic Records or "The Book of Life" can be equated to the universe's super computer system. It is this system that acts as the central storehouse of all information for every individual who has ever lived upon the Earth. More than just a reservoir of events, the Akashic Records contain every deed, word, feeling, thought, and intent that has ever occurred at any time in the history of the world. Much more than simply a memory storehouse, however, these Akashic Records are interactive in that they have a tremendous influence upon our everyday lives, our relationships, our feelings and belief systems, and the potential realities we draw toward us.

The Akashic Records contain the entire history of every soul since the dawn of Creation. These records connect each one of us to one another. They contain the stimulus for every archetypal symbol or mythic story, which has ever deeply touched patterns of human behaviour and experience. They have been the inspiration for dreams and invention. They draw us toward or repel us from one another. They mold and shape levels of human consciousness and are a portion of Divine Mind. They are the unbiased judge and jury that attempt to guide, educate, and transform every individual to become the very best that she or he can be. They embody an ever-changing fluid array of possible futures that are called into potential as humans interact and learn from the data that has already been accumulated.

Alpha:

Brain wave measurement and activity of 8 - 13 cps cycles per second; a state of being deeply relaxed, passive but aware, composed, it is the state of waking and just before sleep and hence is the perfect programming time. Alpha is the early meditative state, entry pattern to begin to access inter-dimensional doors to higher consciousness. Also measured or seen as integrated hemispheric brain function and subconscious mind/brain function.

Arcturian System:

Located in Bootes Constellation, in this context we look at fifth dimensional life and above.

Ayahuasca (Sacred Tea):

Held in high esteem by many South American indigenous, Ayahuasca is said to be the most Sacred Power Plant teacher of the psychotropic plants. Found in the jungles of South America it is often used ritualistically by Shaman to explore the inter-dimensional worlds. Made from the jagube vine, and also the chacruna leaf, to represent the yang and yin of life, when the two are harvested and mixed, using ancient rituals, a Sacred Tea is formed. Many claim that when taken this tea awakens the Christed Light within and strips the veils of illusion that separate the inner plane realms

Beta:

Beta if the general field of mass consciousness. Brain wave patterns in Beta 1 are at 14 to 20 cycles per second; and in Beta at 2 - 20 to 40 cps. This is a state of being fully awake, alert, excited, tense and also sometimes speedy, not 'centered'. In this busy brain wave pattern human beings are held in limitation.

Delta:

The brain wave pattern that runs between 0.5 to 3 cps. Delta is a slow wave pattern and signature frequency of the brainstem and it is seen as a deep sleep state or the ultimate reality - 'beyond mind' meditation. Delta range frequencies trigger healing and rejuvenation and are said to open the gateway to 'satori' or enlightenment and quantum consciousness.

DOW – Divine One Within – in this book called Essence.

The all-powerful, all loving, all wise, all knowing energy force that dwells in every atom. Our Superior Self or Christed nature, the higher aspect of ourselves that guides, loves, heals, inspires us all.

Dreamtime:

Based in Australian Aboriginal legend, where it is a field from which all life is created.

Enchanted Kingdom:
A world that represents the best of the human heart and dreaming, "The Enchanted Kingdom was a land of an ancient space held in a field beyond time, a place that seemed like a layer of life wedged between worlds. Hosho had described it as a realm outside of time, a field of possibilities where everything was possible for the dream weavers and the wise."

Essence Extensions:
Light rays of intelligence from the Great Central Sun Beings that take embodiment in different ways. Applies to all people on earth.

Etheric Form:
The energy field of light, around which molecular structure is attracted, seen by some as a light-body around which our physical form is developed.

Federation Academy:
Place of training for the Cosmic Knights.

Intergalactic Federation of Worlds:
A peace focused type of futuristic 'Cosmic United Nations' council that act on a Universal and inter-dimensional level to oversee the harmonious awakening and integration of evolving worlds.

Field Fiddlers:
Awakened ones trained or in training to harmonize the worlds.

Harmony Code:
A code of intention and action used to harmonize the fields and deliver beneficial outcomes for all.

The Matrix:
Also known as the web of Oneness that rose from the field of love to give life and allow humanity to explore their co-creative powers. Also seen by some to be the web of Christed Consciousness, and by others to be the field that contains the Buddha's Pure Land, or where we can experience Samadhi.

Rainbow Serpent:
Known in aboriginal culture to represent the return of the higher nature within us and the rising within us of our more enlightened nature.

Redemption:

In this context, the process of transformation where we exhibit and operate from our more ascended nature.

Sacred Plants/Tea research: see Ayahuasca. Read Visions of the Forest by Alex Polari de Alverga

Shamballa, Shambhala:

Also known as Elysium, El Dorado, Eden or Shangri-la – a state of heaven-like reality where the highest of humanity is made manifest and the DOW (Divine One Within) is awake and guiding all and our lower nature is DOW merged.

We invite you to research the Internet for different views on the myths of Shamballa and also to meditate on the Shamballa reality and see what unfolds for you.

Soul Splits:

See Michael Newton's Journey of Souls and Destiny of Souls research.

The Theta Field:

Theta brain wave patterns are between 4 - 7 cps and these occur as we go into deep meditation. Theta is the drowsy, waking dream state, associated with higher feeling states. Gateway to learning and memory, it is also the increased state of creativity and intuition. Subliminal conscious states of ESP, channeling, insight and profound understanding of just knowing that come to those who reach the theta levels in meditation.

Walk-In:

In the context of Book 2, a walk-in is a disembodied spirit that takes over a healthy body when the existing soul within it no longer wants to stay. An exchange made as a positive mutual agreement. Ruth Montgomery author of *Strangers Among Us* discusses this in greater detail.

For further data on any other subject of interest in this series, we recommend you sit in silence and meditate upon it and also search the innernet and also the internet and use your intuitive discernment.

About the Enchanted Kingdom series ....

The Enchanted Kingdom is a land of an ancient space held in a field beyond time, a place that seems like a layer of life wedged between worlds. The alchemists describe it as a field of possibilities where everything is available for the dreamtime dancers and the wise. A parallel world dreamt into being over millennia by those seeking higher worlds, the Enchanted Kingdom represents the highest visions and dreams of humankind. And now, finally, this Kingdom is merging with Earth's own world.

Also available:- The Enchanted Kingdom Trilogy - 3 books in one.
Three books in one to form a most uplifting trilogy by metaphysical author Jasmuheen. Queen of the Matrix – Fiddlers of the Fields; King of Hearts – The Field of Love; and Elysium – Shamballa's Sacred Symphony. The Elysium prophecy states:- When the Queen of the Matrix returns the King to her heart, peace will come to all on Earth, regardless of their part. And when compassion sets the pace, all will find new rhythms, a peace within, and a peace without, to last beyond millenniums. A cross between Harry Potter, Star Wars & the Matrix movies, this new trilogy of fiction weaves in some of the aboriginal dreamtime legends while offering insights on past lives and future lives; perfect love and profound love plus parallel worlds. All of this is covered in this enchanting trilogy, which will enlighten and entertain all ages.
- Print: $55.00 (3 books in one 680 page volume - to be mailed to you); Download: $33.00
- **http://www.lulu.com/content/2453011** to order and also read a few chapters.

You can also enjoy the first three books in the series as separate books.

QUEEN OF THE MATRIX - **Fiddlers of the Fields with Jasmuheen (book 1 in the Enchanted Kingdom Trilogy)**
In book one of this trilogy we find the master field fiddler Tan living on board the Starship Elysium with Rani and those who oversee the merging of the realms. The Starship Elysium has detected an anomaly

in the Matrix that has begun to bleed through into future worlds and alter the course of the merging. Now the Queen's light is dimming and the witch must be reborn to close the doors to the darker worlds while Tan seeks to contain the damage.

Decades before Tan and Rani had found themselves as young children sent backwards in time to be held in a field of Enchantment. Watched over by Shadow, the she-wolf, and Crystalina a field surfing fairy, they encounter both evil and the mesmerizing magic of paradise worlds at play as they battle their wills with the witch and the warlock who is her long-time mate. Now they must return to the enchanted realm to find the keys to deal with a new breed of Artificial Intelligence that treats humanity as a virus to eradicate. Trained at the Cadet's Space Station in the art of fiddling the fields, Tan goes back in time to reprogram the A.I. systems before the anomaly of their terrifying reign can begin. Connecting with powerful shaman and dreamtime guides, these time travelling fiddlers of the fields are supported by the ancient alchemists and the Lady of Light, as they discover the secrets of the merging.

- Print: $22.00 (to be mailed to you); Download: $11.00 from lulu.com:
- **http://www.lulu.com/content/1763090** to order and also read a few chapters.

Worlds of enchantment, merging with worlds of chaos and pain.
Witches and warlocks redeemed and made whole again.
Wise Ones and mentors to keep the players sane.
Stories, tools and insights with so much more to gain.
Addictions and dreaming with lives lived on other planes.
Kings of Hearts and Queens seeking to lovingly reign.

KING OF HEARTS - The Field of Love - with Jasmuheen (book 2 in the Enchanted Kingdom Trilogy)

The King was in his counting house, counting all his blessings.
The Queen was in the parlor in prayer and still guessing.
Sweet girls were in the garden, their young men close behind,

the Matrix was now pulsing as love bloomed through life's vine.

Past lives, future lives and the perfect moments of the present; perfect love, profound love and painful plus parallel worlds and the art of dream weaving ... all of this is covered in book 2 of the Enchanted Kingdom Series as the Queen of the Matrix calls the King of Hearts to rise. In book one of this series, we witnessed the redemption of dark hearts with Agra's journey back to the Garden of Isis plus Tan's quest to reprogram the Terradac's codes. In this book, we discover the gypsy Jacob and his journey of transformation with a walk-in warlock as they deal with the Dark Ones of power and find the risen King. Via the stories of Tan and Rani; Loki and Aphrodite plus Mary and Leila, we expand on the both the ancient art of sexual tantra and the depth and weaves of love's fields with its layers of loss and the joy of dream's made whole. Again, we explore the complexity of metaphysical realities of multi-dimensional realms and share more of the ancient wisdom as it applies to the field of love.

- Print: $22.00 (to be mailed to you); Download: $11.00 from lulu.com:
- **http://www.lulu.com/content/2445645** to order and also read a few chapters.

ELYSIUM - Shamballa's Sacred Symphony with Jasmuheen (book 3 in the Enchanted Kingdom Trilogy)

The third book in the Enchanted Kingdom Trilogy, ELYSIUM continues the story of Rani and Tan as they discover the pathways to Shamballa and develop the Heartland Game. Tracked by both the Dark Ones as well as other Alchemists that are also focused on the merging of the worlds, in this book we cover the movement of the rapture, Shamballa's Shadowlands, parallel worlds plus Earth's rise into more civilized realms. Guided by the futuristic Commander of the Starship Elysium we also track the story of the immortal monk Tao Lao who moves back in time to work with Isabella and influence a young bomber who is hell bent on revenge.

As with the first two books, 'Queen of the Matrix' and 'The King of Hearts', in Elysium we again find stories of love and hardship and change that are interspersed with esoteric insights to support the rising of Earth into higher realms.

Shamballa's sacred symphony is crossing time and space,
  forming new realities that are led by waves of grace.
 Now Elysium is rising as freedom's path is laid,
  by those who know how true love's beat is made.

A cross between Harry Potter, Star Wars & the Matrix movies, this new trilogy of fiction also weaves in some of the aboriginal dreamtime legends while offering powerful metaphysical tools and futuristic insights that will entertain and enlighten all ages.

- Print: $22.00 (to be mailed to you); Download: $11.00 from lulu.com:
- **http://www.lulu.com/content/2445744** to order and read a few chapters.

Cosmic Wanderers – Homeward Bound

In "Cosmic Wanderers – Homeward Bound" story-teller Jasmuheen brings it all to the Universal stage, to address intergalactic warfare, Earth as a garden of Eden, her future and past, plus prophecy & global change.

Sharing accepted spiritual intelligence in an entertaining way, Jasmuheen provides in-depth information on U.F.O.'s, walk-ins, abductions,inter-dimensional life & Beings of Light, Essence extensions of the Great Central Sun, E.T. genetic manipulation, the alchemy of futuristic science regarding worlds ascending and the metaphysics of peace for all.

Entwining the ongoing love stories of 8tlan, Tao Lao, Rani, Tan and other well-loved characters in this series, ancient esoteric wisdoms are revealed that are so relevant to Earth today.

It is not necessary to have read the previous booksin the Enchanted Kingdom series, to enjoy and appreciate all that this new book in the EK series"Cosmic Wanderers - Homeward Bound" contains.

The Enchanted Kingdom series is said by many to be a cross between Harry Potter and Star Wars while proving deep esoteric truths about creation!

JASMUHEEN
Biography & Background
www.jasmuheen.com

Jasmuheen's main service agenda is the raising of consciousness to create a healthy, harmonious world. To support this she is the author of 33 metaphysical books that are published in 18 languages; the Founder of the Embassy of Peace and implementer of its Personal, Global & Universal Harmonization Projects; she is also an Ambassador of Peace for the Madonna Frequency Planetary Peace Program; Pranic Living & eliminating global hunger; international lecturer on metaphysics, ascension & interdimensional energy field science. Jasmuheen is also a leading researcher on the controversial pranic nourishment reality & Darkroom Training facilitator; founder of the Self Empowerment Academy; facilitator of the C.I.A. – the Cosmic Internet Academy; publisher & film-maker; artist presenting Sacred Art Retreats, musician & President of the Global Congress – Pyramid Valley, Bangalore, India.

On Pranic Living Jasmuheen writes: "Pranic Living is not a diet - it is an ascension into more refined evolutionary paths on both individual then global levels! As vast multi-dimensional beings, we have limitless access to a source of internal nourishment (prana-chi) that constantly bubbles champagne-like throughout the matrix of life. This pranic stream acts as a type of glue to bind our creations and help with our manifestations to bring more Grace into our lives. Meditation allows us to go deep within the inner silence to discover and experience this pranic flow in all its forms and as we focus upon it we become immersed within it and so find ourselves ascended and transformed. Increasing our personal internal & external chi flow like we do in our gatherings and retreats can rid our world of all of all its hungers and bring about a state of global harmony and permanent peace and so our international tours seminars and retreats continue with this focus."

As many are now aware, metaphysical author Jasmuheen has spent the last four decades studying the rhythms of the field of Divine Love to the degree that in 1993 she discovered its ability to provide nourishment on not just emotional, mental and spiritual levels but also on a physical level. She then toured extensively sharing this with all those open to experience this different way of being nourished, continually also offering deep meditations within the field of love that will align us more powerfully to this nourishing force so that our presence enhances human evolution in ways that benefit us all. Pranic living then gave birth to the Embassy of Peace with its pragmatic Programs & Projects of Personal, Global & Universal Harmonization.

JASMUHEEN'S BACKGROUND Timeline

❖ 1957 – Born in Australia to Norwegian immigrants

❖ 1959 – Began focus on vegetarianism

❖ 1964 – Began to study Chi

❖ 1971 – Discovered the Languages of Light

❖ 1974 – Initiated into Ancient Vedic Meditation and eastern philosophy

❖ 1974 – Began periodic fasting

❖ 1974 – Discovered telepathic abilities

❖ 1975 - 1992 – Raised children, studied and applied metaphysics, enjoyed a 10 year career in finance and computer programming

❖ 1992 – Retired from the corporate world to pursue metaphysical life

❖ 1992 – Met many Masters of Alchemy including those from the Great White Brotherhood the Higher Light Scientists from Arcturius and the Intergalactic Federation of World's Council

❖ 1993 – Underwent the Prana Initiation to increase her chi flow and began to live on light

❖ 1994 – Began an intensive 14 year research project on Divine Nutrition and pranic nourishment

❖ 1994 – Began her global service agenda with the Ascended Masters

❖ 1994 – Received the first of 5 volumes of channeled messages from the Ascended Masters

❖ 1994 – Wrote the metaphsyical manual *In Resonance*

❖ 1994 – Founded the Self Empowerment Academy in Australia

❖ 1994 – Began to hold classes in metaphysics and Self Mastery

❖ 1994 – Began *The Art of Resonance* newsletter renamed later as *The ELRAANIS Voice*

❖ 1995 – Traveled extensively around Australia, Asia and New Zealand sharing Self-Mastery research

❖ 1995 – Wrote *Pranic Nourishment (Living on Light) – Nutrition for the New Millennium*

❖ 1996 – Invited to present the Pranic Nourishment research to the Global stage

❖ 1996 – Began an intensive re-education program with the Global Media

❖ 1996 – Set up the International M.A.P.S. Ambassadry – Established in 33 countries

❖ 1996 – Created the *C.I.A. – the Cosmic Internet Academy* – a free website to download data for positive personal and planetary progression. Web address:

❖ www.selfempowermentacademy.com.au

❖ 1996 - 2001 – Traveled extensively to Europe, the U.K., the U.S.A. and Brazil with the '*Back to Paradise*' agenda

❖ 1996 - 2004 – Talked about Divine Power and Divine Nutrition to > 900 million via the global media

- 1997 – Began to set up scientific research project for Living on Light
- 1997 – Began the *Our Camelot Trilogy*, wrote *The Game of Divine Alchemy*
- 1997 – Formed the M.A.P.S. Ambassadry Alliance – people committed to global harmony and peace
- 1998 – International tour to share the Impeccable Mastery Agenda
- 1998 – Wrote *Our Progeny – the X-Re-Generation*
- 1999 – Wrote the *Wizard's Tool Box* which later became the *Biofields and Bliss* Series.
- 1999 – Wrote *Dancing with my DOW : Media Mania, Mastery and Mirth*
- 1998 - 1999 – Wrote and published *Ambassadors of Light – World Health World Hunger Project*
- 1999 – Began contacting World Governments regarding Hunger and Health Solutions
- 1999 – International tour to share the Blueprint for Paradise
- 1999 - 2001 – Began M.A.P.S. Ambassadors International Training Retreats
- 2000 – International tour '*Dancing with the Divine*' to facilitate the election of an Etheric Government in 28 key cities and also shared the Luscious Lifestyles Program – L.L.P.
- 2000 - 2001 – Wrote *Cruising Into Paradise* an esoteric coffee table book
- 1999 - 2001 – Wrote *Divine Radiance – On the Road with the Masters of Magic* and
- 2001 – Wrote *Four Body Fitness : Biofields and Bliss* Book 1
- 2000 - 2001 – Launched the OPHOP agenda One People in Harmony on One Planet
- 2001 – Wrote the book *Co-Creating Paradise : Biofields and Bliss* Book 2
- 2001 – Launched Recipe 2000> as a tool to co-create global health and happiness; peace and prosperity for all on Earth
- 2002 – Launched www.jasmuheen.com with its Perfect Alignment Perfect Action Holistic Education Programs; and its I.R.S. focus to Instigate, Record and Summarize humanity's co-creation of paradise.
- 2002 – Did the 'Divine Radiance FOUR BODY FITNESS – Unity 2002' World Tour
- 2002 – Received, wrote and launched *The Madonna Frequency Planetary Peace Program* as the free e-Book, Biofields and Bliss Book 3.
- 2002 - 2003 – Wrote *The Food of Gods*.
- 2003 – World Tour "Divine Nutrition and The Madonna Frequency Planetary Peace Project".
- 2004 – Wrote *The Law of Love* then toured with "The Law of Love and

Its Fabulous Frequency of Freedom" agenda.

❖ 2005 – Wrote *Harmonious Healing and The Immortals Way*, then toured with the "Harmonious Healing" agenda.

❖ 2005 – Began work on The Freedom of the Immortals Way plus continued with writing *The Enchanted Kingdom* Trilogy & *The Prana Program* for Third World Countries.

❖ 2005 – Presented THE PRANA PROGRAM to the Society for Conscious Living at the United Nations in Vienna – Nov. 2005

❖ 2006 – International tour with THE PRANA PROGRAM

❖ 2007 – International tour focus on THE SECOND COMING and SECOND CHANCE DANCES.

❖ 2007 – Launched THE EMBASSY OF PEACE on 07-07-07 & began training programs for Ambassadors of Peace & Diplomats of Love.

❖ 2007 – Released the book *The Bliss of Brazil & The Second Coming*

❖ 2008 – Released *The Enchanted Kingdom* Series after 6 years of writing *The Queen of the Matrix, The King of Hearts* and *Elysium*.

❖ 2008 - Toured with the Future Worlds Future Humans agenda and begins more intense work in India.

❖ 2008 – Appointed President of the Global Congress of Spiritual Scientists Pyramid valley, Bangalore India.

❖ 2008 – Released the coffee table books *Sacred Scenes & Visionary Verse* plus *Cruising Into Paradise*.

❖ 2009 – Released and toured with the *Universal Harmonization Program* for the Embassy of Peace, focusing on research into extraterrestrial intelligence.

❖ 2009 – Released her book *Meditation Magic*

❖ 2009 – Began writing *Cosmic Wanderers* – book 4 in the Enchanted Kingdom series

❖ 2010 – Jasmuheen continues her work in South America and India and tours with the Harmonics of the Heavenly Heart & Pranic Living Agenda

❖ 2010 – From 2009 to 2011 Jasmuheen focused on providing free VIDEOs for education & entertainment on her YouTube Channel, plus creating education DVD's, art & music. Jasmuheen's YouTube channel now has over 480 free educational videos - http://youtube.com/jasmuheen

❖ 2011 – Released her *Pathways of Peace Pragmatics* book then toured and offered her YouTube videos on this.

❖ 2011 – *Siriana's Adventures – Earth Bound* book released. The first in her new children's series.

❖ 2012 – Jasmuheen released her *Being Essence* booklet and this was the focus of her world tour. She also completed her *Cosmic Wanderers* book and her travel journal *The Rhythms of Love*. Both released towards the end of 2012.

❖ In 2013 her focus continues on *Peace Paradigms and Programs.*

Jasmuheen's books are now published in 18 languages.

BOOKS BY JASMUHEEN

A selection of JASMUHEEN'S research manuals can also be purchased from http://www.jasmuheen.com/products-page/

1) THE ENCHANTED KINGDOM Trilogy - 3 books in one.
2) QUEEN OF THE MATRIX - Fiddlers of the Fields with Jasmuheen (book 1 in the Enchanted Kingdom Trilogy)
3) KING OF HEARTS - The Field of Love - with Jasmuheen (book 2 in the Enchanted Kingdom Trilogy)
4) ELYSIUM - Shamballa's Sacred Symphony with Jasmuheen (book 3 in the Enchanted Kingdom Trilogy)
5) The Food of Gods
6) The Law of Love & Its Fabulous Frequency of Freedom
7) THE PRANA PROGRAM - Effective & Enjoyable Evolution
8) PRANIC NOURISHMENT - Nutrition for the New Millennium
9) Ambassadors of Light : World Health World Hunger Project
10) The Bliss of Brazil & The Second Coming
11) In Resonance
12) Divine Radiance - On the Road with the Masters of Magic
13) HARMONIOUS HEALING & The Immortal's Way with Jasmuheen.
14) Darkroom Diary Downloads & The Freedom of The Immortal's Way
15) Cosmic Colleagues – Messages from the Masters
16) Biofields & Bliss Trilogy
17) Four Body Fitness : Biofields & Bliss
18) Co-creating Paradise
19) 'The Madonna Frequency' Planetary Peace Program'
20) Meditation Magic
21) Sacred Scenes & Visionary Verse
22) Cruising Into Paradise
23) Embassy of Peace Programs
24) Siriana's Adventures – Earth Bound
25) Pathways of Peace
26) Being Essence
27) Cosmic Wanderers – book 4 in the Enchanted Kingdom series

Made in the USA
Middletown, DE
31 October 2020

23078287R00097